THE BLOOD TIDE

A Scott Stiletto Thriller 7

BRIAN DRAKE

WOLFPACK
PUBLISHING
— EST 2013 —

Published in the United States by Wolfpack Publishing, Las Vegas

Wolfpack Publishing
6032 Wheat Penny Avenue
Las Vegas, NV 89122

wolfpackpublishing.com

Paperback ISBN 978-1-64734-002-5
eBook ISBN 978-1-64734-001-8

Library of Congress Number:2019956873

THE BLOOD TIDE

CHAPTER ONE

Somewhere in Washington, DC

The dark-haired man wearing a leather jacket stepped into the elevator and avoided eye contact. Scott Stiletto, leaning against the right wall of the elevator car, watched him, noting his strong build, and that the leather jacket was too large and unzipped. *There's a gun under there.*

Pressing a button for a floor below the selection Scott had made, the elevator doors rumbled closed, but not before the specter of the Grim Reaper also stepped inside, and a chill crawled up Stiletto's neck. He'd be dead in the next few seconds unless he acted quickly.

Scott shifted his weight and waited for the killer to strike. As the elevator climbed upward, the indicator lights above the door flashed as they passed each floor, the killer's right hand flashed under his coat, coming out in a quick arc with a suppressed Browning .22 pistol in his fist.

Stiletto knew the weapon. The Buck Mark, one of the finest .22 semi-automatic handguns available, and the favored weapon of assassins who liked to get close. The Mossad had perfected .22-caliber assassinations, and whoever trained the killer had taught him the same technique.

The ugly snout of the suppressor displayed a small, but deeply black, hole at the end, from which a full metal jacket projectile would emerge at the twitch of the killer's index finger.

The killer may have had a good teacher, but his execution was flawed. His biggest mistake was fully extending his arm. Stiletto used that mistake to his advantage.

Scott's left hand flashed up, grasping the killer's wrist, twisting hard. As the assassin cried out at the sudden torque turning his arm in a direction it wasn't designed to go, Scott snapped his left leg out, the heel of his shoe landing solidly against the killer's right knee. The joint snapped, the killer losing his balance, Stiletto pivoted to deliver a crushing right fist into the man's jaw. Wrenching the Browning pistol from the killer's hand, cracking the man's index finger in the process, Stiletto grasped the pistol in his right hand and shot the killer three times in the head, each .22 slug punching through bone and sending brain-shattering shockwaves through his skull.

The assassin's body fell in a heap. Scott, breathing hard, tossed the pistol beside the man.

The elevator stopped. Stiletto stood still as the doors

slid open, but nobody waited on the other side. The last thing he needed were panicked witnesses. The hotel cameras were bad enough. There was no way he'd get out without being photographed, and if police looked for anybody hurriedly exiting the building around the time of the shooting, he'd be picked up for sure.

Whoever discovered the body would scream loud, and by the time that happened, Scott planned to be well away from the hotel.

He raced out of the elevator and hurried down the empty hallway at a trot, the key card already in his hand. He switched the card to his left while reaching under his own jacket for his gun. He had no suppressor on the barrel, but that didn't matter now. If the killer had back-up waiting in the room, in the case of failure, Stiletto wasn't going to waste time trying to be quiet.

He stopped at the plain brown door with the number 608 in gold numbering, still panting, but taking deep breaths to try and calm down.

The Russians. No doubt.

Somehow, they had tracked him to Washington, DC.

The *how* wasn't Stiletto's concern. His only goal was survival and escape.

The lock clicked and Stiletto pushed open the door with the Colt .45 leading the way.

Nobody waited for him.

Scott pushed the door shut, engaged the lock, and flipped the security catch. Putting his gun away, he pulled out his cell and dialed while pacing, still trying to catch his breath. The adrenaline charge had been huge. Stiletto had enjoyed his much needed peace and quiet in recent weeks, but the killer had shattered that peace.

He held the phone to his ear and waited.

"Yes?" The voice of an old man Stiletto knew as Number One, the leader of a private intelligence organization called The Trust, was welcome.

"It's Scott."

"What is it?"

"They found me," Stiletto said. "I'm blown. I need help getting out of here."

"Where are you?"

"The hotel we talked about."

"Get on the street and keep moving. I'll call back with an address. Somebody will pick you up."

"It has to be somebody I recognize. Is Beth Carrington available?"

Beth, a Trust operative, had worked with Stiletto on an assignment in Venezuela. Their association had started out antagonistic, their personalities and approaches to work polar opposite, but by the end of the mission, they'd grown to respect each other.

"She's nearby. I'll dispatch her to collect you."

"Thank you."

Stiletto ended the call and jammed the phone in his pocket. He didn't have much, a single suitcase and tote bag. He hurriedly packed and slipped out of the hotel by the East exit and joined pedestrian traffic on the sidewalk, casting furtive glances around him. *It's not paranoia if somebody truly is trying to kill you.* He'd call the hotel later and check-out by phone when he was secured where assassins couldn't reach him.

But as long as the Russian kill contract remained open, Stiletto knew safe havens would grow fewer and farther between.

The Kremlin had placed a contract on Stiletto's life for an illegal mission into Moscow several months earlier, and there had been a target on his back ever since.

The recent peace and quiet had lulled Stiletto into a false sense of security. He was in Washington to end his freelance status, and officially become a member of The Trust after earlier refusing the offer. Number One promised his influence could get the contract cancelled, and the assassin in the elevator proved once and for all that living forever on the run wasn't an option.

Stiletto crossed the street several times, waited in alcoves, checking behind him in a variety of ways, until Number One called with the promised address. Three blocks away. Stiletto headed for the pick-up point. He hoped Number One had the influence he promised. Stiletto wasn't sure how much longer he could survive on his own.

CHAPTER TWO

Stiletto recognized Beth Carrington as she stopped curb-side in a black Lincoln Continental. He dropped his suit-case and tote in the back seat, which looked large enough to house an elephant, and hopped into the passenger seat. She smoothly drove into traffic, the Lincoln's engine very quiet. Stiletto buckled his seat belt.

"You okay?" she said.

"Hanging in there."

He glanced at her. The first time they'd met, she wore a fancy party dress with her hair tied back. This time she wore street clothes, with her hair down, but despite her plain-Jane façade, her sharp blue eyes made her stand out. They were a bright contrast to her otherwise pale skin.

"Boss says it's pretty serious."

"The boss," Stiletto said, "has a knack for understate-ment."

"Russians?"

"I think so."

"Relax. I'm taking you where they won't be able to find you."

"Where?"

"Headquarters. It's going to be a bit of a drive so I hope you went to the bathroom."

Stiletto laughed and wiped the strain off his face. The Lincoln surged ahead as traffic opened, and Stiletto indeed began to relax. The Lincoln had very comfortable seats.

"A regular safe house isn't available?" he said.

"You were going to be taken to our headquarters anyway, but now we're doing it early."

"I'm glad you were available."

"Nuts. I got here a few hours ago. I was supposed to check in at HQ and hang out until you showed up. There's a big job brewing, and we're going to be busy the next few days."

"Really?"

"You think you were coming out here only to talk?" She looked at him, light from a street lamp flashing across her face. "You're on the payroll now, Scott. We aren't an outfit that lets people sit around."

"I can't wait to see this place," Stiletto said.

Beth Carrington left Washington via Highway 66, making the 81 connection south through Harrisburg. She planned to drive all night, which was fine with Stiletto, but they did require a stop along the way. When she finally admitted they were driving deep into the George Washington and Jefferson National Forest, he expressed surprise.

"That's where HQ is?"

"Former farm, yeah. All tricked out with the latest and greatest hardware, underground control center, barracks, everything you need, including a no-fly zone to keep private and commercial air traffic away."

"That indeed sounds like a good place to hide for a while."

They switched mid-way so Beth could grab a cat nap, Stiletto following the GPS most of the way to the forest before pulling over to wake Beth. She told him the way in wasn't on any map and certainly not on GPS.

He settled back into the passenger seat while Beth resumed driving. Presently she turned off the highway, following a winding two-lane highway for a few miles, before taking a turnoff marked Private. The pavement ended, replaced by hard-packed dirt.

"Be glad it's not raining," she said.

The Lincoln handled the dirt road well, rocking here and there as the level of the ground shifted, and presently the tires grabbed pavement again. The road was narrow, Stiletto didn't think two vehicles going opposite directions could pass, but Beth didn't seem concerned. Perhaps, Stiletto decided, this was the road *IN*, and there was another road *OUT*.

He saw nothing out the window other than what the headlamps highlighted, a heavily-forested area, the foliage threatening to retake the paved portion. The road was clear enough that a crew probably tended to the upkeep on a regular schedule.

A barred gate appeared in the beam of lights. Beth slowed to a stop and pressed a button on the dash. The gate swung back, allowing her to pass. She stopped on the other side, pressed the button again, and then continued. Stiletto looked back. In the glare of the rear lights, he watched the gate swing closed.

They stayed on the narrow road another twenty minutes, Stiletto staying quiet to let Beth concentrate.

And then the narrow road opened onto a wide area of flat land, surrounded, by what Stiletto could make out, by mountains. Several buildings dotted the open area, which seemed about the length of two football fields. The Lincoln's headlamps zeroed on barracks buildings, because nothing else on earth is built like a barracks.

"I'm getting flashbacks to my army days."

"Drill sergeant yell at you a lot?"

"He always told me I'd make a great shoe salesman after I got out of the army."

"I don't get it."

"*Stiletto.*"

"Oh." She laughed. "That's funny."

Stiletto smiled. Maybe he should have followed Sergeant Guzman's advice. *If only* . . .

The field was carefully maintained, with several buildings in the unmistakable shape of barracks, three in a row, and then a separate building off to one side. A cluster of cars were neatly parked near the barracks. They passed by and headed for another building about thirty yards away, this one a little larger. It looked like a colonial-style home, at least two stories, white with columns holding up the second level awning.

"This place is very unassuming," Stiletto said. "You said the works were underground?"

"State of the art facility, yup. This looks boring for a reason."

As they neared the Colonial, which Beth explained was the main office, Stiletto noticed the silhouette of a man standing at the top of the steps leading to the front door.

The profile of the man struck Stiletto's memory. His gut told him he'd seen the figure many times before, but his mind refused to accept the assumed identity.

"You okay?" Beth said.

Stiletto said nothing. Beth stopped the car in front of the building and Scott exited quickly.

The man stepped forward, into the brightness of the security light in front of the building, and Scott froze.

The man on the porch was named Fleming.

"General" Isaac Fleming. Stiletto's old boss at the CIA.

CHAPTER THREE

"Hello, Scott."

Stiletto said, "I don't believe it."

"It's me." Fleming, wearing a suit that looked wrinkled enough to have been worn all day, stepped off the porch and greeted Stiletto with a warm handshake that turned into a brief embrace.

"What are you doing here?" Stiletto said, adding, "Sir?" out of habit.

"It's a bit of a story, which we'll get to, but I understand you've had some trouble."

"I don't know where to start."

Beth Carrington collected Stiletto's bags from the back seat and set them beside him. He thanked her.

"Let's go inside and talk about it," the General said. He turned to Beth. "Miss Carrington, thank you for bringing Scott here."

"I'm turning in," she said. "See you tomorrow." She

turned the car around and headed for one of the barracks separated from the row of three, parking alongside another line of cars.

Stiletto turned back to General Ike. He had no words as he took in the sight of the man who had been like a father to him at CIA, a tough task-master, yet also one who understood that he had to take care of his people if they were going to perform at the top of their game.

"Come on," Fleming said. Stiletto grabbed his luggage and followed the man inside the building.

Fleming's office was on the top floor. They took the stairs. The colonial motif continued inside, lots of white, wainscoting, and red carpet on the steps. Questions crowded Stiletto's mind, but he knew the answers were forthcoming. General Ike had told him, at the end of the Russian misadventure, that he'd been part of The Trust for some time, and had, in fact, tipped Number One to the fact that Stiletto needed help in Moscow. The General's membership wasn't a question. Stiletto wanted to know why he wasn't at CIA any longer.

General Ike stepped into a large office with a window that surely had a great view of the field during the day, but the darkness outside was the only view now. The General offered Stiletto the seat in front of his desk, and Stiletto, with a terrific sense of déjà vu, placed his bags on the floor and sat down.

And there was no doubt that Fleming had firmly cemented his presence in the office. Having earned the

"General" nickname because of his long army career, Fleming's preferred office decorations were 1700-vintage navy ships, with models and paintings on the walls depicting such craft. Stiletto had always wondered what contributed to General Ike's preference for naval art, but had never asked.

And some things never changed, such as the General's habit of not having any family pictures on his desk, but Scott knew he'd been married to the same woman for almost forty years. He had sharp blue eyes and dark hair, and a scar on his right cheek. There had been much speculation about how the General had acquired that scar back at CIA, and it was another story Fleming never told. Those blue eyes bored into Stiletto as they always had prior to a discussion, and they were a great comfort to Scott.

"I know it's late," Fleming said, "and you're probably exhausted, but let me get you up to speed and then you can crash for the night because we'll be even busier in the coming days."

Stiletto crossed his legs and waited.

"We had a blow-out at CIA," Fleming said. "Have you heard?"

"I haven't," Stiletto said.

"You may remember certain opponents our department had on the Senate Intelligence Committee."

Stiletto did. General Fleming had been in charge of the Special Activities Division, the Agency "skull smashers" trusted with covert missions. Certain senators on the

Intelligence Committee never liked how Fleming did his job or ran his department, and used every opportunity to call his judgement into question, with the threat to refuse funding if he didn't explain himself. Fleming had managed to dodge every bullet the committee fired, but it seemed his luck had finally run out.

"They managed to get rid of me, after a series of disasters, which, of course, they blamed on me."

"What happened?"

"We were running an anti-drug operation in Colombia, and we were exposed before it started. We lost some good people. And we missed out on a primary goal, discovering the cartel's connection in the United States. One cartel in particular has linked up with an east coast mafia interest to help bring drugs into the country. Part of our mission was to find out how they made that connection, but we failed. And, for the life of me, we were not able to track down the leak."

"And they got rid of you?"

Anger flashed behind the General's eyes. "The Intelligence Committee put pressure on the DCI to make changes. The operation had cost millions already, and the choice was to either close it down or get new blood in management. They essentially want their own preferred leadership in charge, they always did, that was the reason for the animosity toward me. Yeah, I got the boot. They'd wanted me gone for some time, and they found their opportunity."

"I know that hurt, sir."

"More than you can imagine. But, luckily, Number One had a job waiting for me, right here."

"What has CIA done about the problem since you left?"

"Paused the program while they try to get the issues sorted. It's been on hold for months. As you can see, I didn't move into this office yesterday."

"Where does The Trust come in?"

"We have taken advantage of the gap to seed our own operatives in Colombia to try and find the answers the CIA can't. Most of the crew worked on the prior operation, so the transition wasn't difficult."

"You have something to prove, don't you, sir?"

"I was accused of being incompetent because I'd grown too comfortable in my position."

"That's a load of crap."

"Thank you, Scott. But the Committee didn't see it that way, and they convinced the DCI. Yes. I have something to prove. These old bones and this old brain of mine can still function properly. We've been betrayed, and we need to know who, why, and how."

"Beth mentioned a big job. Are we going to Colombia?"

"I want you on the team, yes."

Stiletto nodded. "I'm ready to get started, sir."

"Not so fast."

"Excuse me?"

"Number One tells me you've accepted the full-time offer?"

"I have, but he's supposed to get the Russians off my back. They almost got me this afternoon."

"Word will reach the Kremlin to back off, but we may need to push a little before you're free to join the mission."

"How do you mean?"

"Do you have a tux?"

Stiletto admitted he did not.

"You're going to need one. There's an embassy party tomorrow night in DC, and there will be a man there that you need to share some words with."

Stiletto said nothing as a wave of tiredness finally swept over him. He felt like he was on a roller coaster, and hoped, soon, that the ride settled. At least a little.

"What am I supposed to say to him, sir?"

Fleming rose from the chair. "We'll talk more tomorrow. Let's get you in a bunk so you can rest and we'll start again when the sun comes up."

Stiletto remained seated. He took a deep breath.

The General sat down again. "Something on your mind?"

"Yes, sir."

"Let's hear it."

Stiletto hesitated, but finally pushed the words out. "About Moscow."

"Uh-huh."

"I'm sorry."

"It's okay."

"I let you down."

"No, you didn't. You'd have let me down if you followed orders and refused to be who you are," the General said. "That's why I assisted in what little way I could, because you were right. The Agency was wrong. It was wrong for its own reasons, and we can debate that another time, but you couldn't have refused to help your friend. That's what makes you better than most. You're not a machine. To treat you like one is a mistake."

Stiletto nodded.

"Is that all?"

"I think so, sir."

The General stood up again. This time, Stiletto rose as well. They walked to the door.

"The only way you can disappoint me," General Ike said, giving Stiletto a squeeze around the shoulders, "is to forget who you are."

"I won't," Stiletto said.

CHAPTER FOUR

The trio of barracks buildings, Fleming explained, were for the security force. The force was made up of members of a private military contracting firm the Trust employed. Most were former US servicemen, hardened fighters with years of experience thanks to American policy overseas.

They patrolled the grounds and the perimeter and practiced in the open field. The other barracks buildings contained two levels of small studio apartments for agents on what Fleming described as "mission rotation". First floor was where the women lived; men on the top. General Ike showed Stiletto into an apartment on the second floor that already had his name on the door.

The space contained a bed, bathroom, small cooking area in a corner, and told him to sack out and they'd talk more in the morning. Stiletto followed orders and passed out on the very comfortable queen bed, feeling more at ease than he had in months. He was home in the US, not in his apartment in Paris; he was with friends, and nothing could hurt him while at this remote outpost used by The Trust.

Stiletto reflected on the conversation he'd had with the General, with one point in particular nagging at him. What did they need him to attend an embassy party for?

With that, he fell asleep.

He awoke the next morning with the sun streaming through the apartment window. He rose thinking he was back in his college dorm, but luckily, he had no roommate who liked running around without his clothes to contend with. The bathroom was small, but the shower accommodating enough, and he managed to wash without bashing his elbows on the wall or sliding glass doors as he enjoyed the hot spray on his body.

He appreciated General Ike's understanding the night before. Scott hadn't realized how much his decision to sneak into Russia might have affected Fleming. The last thing Scott wanted was to hurt the man, and if he hadn't been so consumed with rescuing a friend who was truly facing the end of his life, with the same threat hanging over his wife and young daughter, Scott might have considered other options. By the time he returned from Russia, their moments together were very brief, as the CIA fired Scott immediately. There had been no time to set things right, or even try.

Stiletto would never forget how General Ike picked him up when he was down, and made him feel useful again.

After retiring from the army, Scott had planned to settle down with his wife and adult daughter and take a cushy security job, but then his wife passed away, and his daughter refused to have anything further to do with him. At loose ends, he accepted a friend's invitation to apply at the CIA.

Over six months, Stiletto participated in a series of exhausting interviews and background checks, and then finally reached the CIA's training facility, where he came to the attention of General Ike's Special Activities Division.

From the first day of his recruitment, Fleming helped Stiletto find his purpose again, and, along with other SAD compatriots, filled a void in Scott's life.

And he'd thrown it all away in exchange for loneliness and a target on his back. He had a chance to regain what he'd lost with the Trust. It was an opportunity he wasn't going to screw up. Fleming and his colleagues would be counting on him to do his part; he wasn't going to let them down. He wasn't going to let anything happen to them.

Stiletto dressed and wondered about breakfast. He had no food to prepare on the stove, and no transportation to go find a restaurant, or how to get to and from the outpost anyway. The answer arrived with Beth Carrington, who knocked on the door and suggested they go eat. Where? First floor of the main building. Small cafeteria. Those working in the underground facility were able to ride an elevator up to the surface for meals, so the cafeteria always had something hot and ready. Stiletto wanted to see the underground wonder Beth and Fleming referred to, but that could wait till later.

They left the barracks and started across the grass to the main building. The air smelled crisp and clean, birds chirping in the distance, a grounds crew working on the landscaping. Stiletto took in the wide field and the surrounding green for the first time.

"Nice place to work."

"There's a heli pad further out, and deeper in the forest we have training areas for shooting, climbing, that sort of thing," Beth explained. "When you're here, you won't be bored."

"Where are the private military guys the General talks about?"

"Exactly," she said. "They're everywhere. We hardly see them unless one squad is coming in and the other going out."

"Tell me more about 'mission rotation'. What is that?"

"When you're on rotation, you're living on base, and you're standing by for anything that requires our attention. When you're off, you can stay here, or get a place in the city, but when I'm off I usually get a hotel or head home to New Hampshire."

"When do you rotate off?"

"Two weeks on, two off," she said. "If you're lucky. Sometimes missions go longer than two weeks. You know that."

"Sure do," Stiletto said.

In the cafeteria, Stiletto asked for the three-egg breakfast that included hash browns and toast, and used the salt and pepper shakers at the table to season the eggs to his liking. Beth went for a veggie omelet.

They caught up on each other's lives since the Venezuela mission, and Stiletto explained traveling to Twin Falls, Idaho, and his complications in that town which still weighed on him. Beth was sympathetic. The conversation was the first time Stiletto had spoken of his difficulties in Twin Falls, and was glad for her ear. He realized she was truly the first human he'd spoken to since leaving Idaho that wasn't a hotel clerk or shop cashier. Working with The Trust would solve more problems than the Russian issue; he'd finally behave like a normal human again.

By the time they'd finished eating, a heavy-set older man entered the cafeteria and eased into a seat at their table. The man was Number One, leader of The Trust. His hair was white, but his eyes sharp, yet showing his age.

He kept his name a secret, so Stiletto had no idea what to call him, other than "sir". It seemed appropriate enough, and why not? The old man had come to Stiletto's aid in more ways than one since his departure from the CIA.

"Welcome to your new home, Mr. Stiletto," Number One said. As always, he spoke slow, deliberately. He was too old to be in a hurry any longer.

"It's very nice."

"I'm afraid the situation you found yourself in yesterday ruined my introduction plans," the old man said. "I had wanted to bring you here myself, and prepare you for meeting your old boss again."

"Killers tend to ruin a lot of plans, sir."

Beth grinned.

"They do indeed," Number One said. "General Ike will be here shortly, but I wanted to talk to you about the embassy party tonight."

"Should I leave?" Beth said.

"Please stay, Miss Carrington," he told her. "You're going too."

"Another party with him?" she said. "Do I have to tell you how he behaved last time?"

Stiletto smiled when she started to laugh. Their first meeting had certainly been complicated, but only because of Stiletto's sour attitude at the time. With better days ahead, he didn't expect that attitude to return.

"I'm sure you'll work it out," Number One said.

"What's the deal in DC?" Stiletto said.

"I've sent word to the Kremlin that you are now under our protection, that the contract should be lifted, and they *will* comply. They know, in no uncertain terms, that any strike against you will result in retaliation. There are too many Trust representatives in Russia for them not to."

"Okay."

"But because of the odd rogue we know exists, a message of a different kind should be delivered. By you. Personally."

"What do you want me to do?"

Number One smiled. Stiletto figured he had a whopper of a scheme in mind and sat quietly until the old man spoke.

CHAPTER FIVE

"The intelligence you brought back from Moscow regarding the Kremlin's use of the Russian mafia as proxy assassins," Number One said. "Do you still have it?"

"No."

Number One frowned. "Why not?"

"I didn't think I'd need to keep it. The CIA has it all."

"Unfortunate, but not a problem. You're going to tell them you still have it. You're going to tell them that if another attempt is made on your life, that if the contract isn't cancelled with the full weight of Kremlin leadership behind the order, the information will be released."

"Who am I telling?"

"Joseph Pietronov will be at the party," Number One said. "He's the embassy representative for Russian intelligence in the United States."

"Never heard of him."

"He's a recent appointment."

"Okay, so me and Beth go to the party tonight," Stiletto said, "and I tell this chap not to bother me anymore, and then we're off to kick some ass?"

"Succinctly put, Mr. Stiletto."

"Thank you, sir. One other question."

"Go ahead."

"Why am I going to this party if you've already told the Kremlin to back off?"

Number One cracked a half smile. "You'll know why once the deed is done, Mr. Stiletto."

Stiletto didn't know what to say to that. Number One took advantage of his pause and excused himself, leaving the table. Scott turned to Beth and sighed.

"I think I know what he has in mind," Beth said.

"Really?"

"Let's go to the party and find out."

Washington, DC

Stiletto glanced at Beth Carrington. The young woman was seated beside him in the back of a long black limousine. They were in the middle of a long line of similar vehicles waiting to deposit passengers at the Russian Embassy on Wisconsin Avenue. Flood lights lit the tall white building, which was partially visible through the tinted windows.

"Are you nervous?" she said.

"Maybe a little," he said.

"Try and relax. We'll only be here long enough to talk to what's-his-face."

"Joseph Pietronov," Stiletto said.

"Memorized his face?"

"I'll know him when I see him."

There were two lines into the ballroom, one that took VIPs through a reception line to meet the Russian officials, and one that didn't. The invitations issued to Stiletto and Beth had been created from scratch by the technical crew at Trust HQ, a room full of quiet engineering types who spent their days perfecting gizmos, gadgets, and methods of mass destruction contained on the point of a needle. They looked legitimate enough to Scott, who only assumed the tech crew had looked at an original in order to make a duplicate.

The fabulously-decorated ballroom shimmered with crystal chandeliers and gold-trimmed draperies. The tiled floor was polished mirror-bright. The ballroom was full of men in tuxedos and women in gowns. A band played soft music, while waiters and waitresses slipped through the crowd with trays of hors d'oeuvres and adult beverages. Stiletto grabbed two martinis from a passing waiter and handed one to Beth. She took a sip.

"Where's your man?" she said.

"He's around," Stiletto said. "Maybe in the line. Let's hang out and look around."

They stood around, drinks in hand, catching pieces of conversations, the diplomats talking off the record, the slightly drunken dance floor activity.

Stiletto finally spotted Joseph Pietronov when he stepped up to the bar, leaning close to the bartender to ask for his order. The bartender listened carefully to the instructions, and began grabbing glasses and bottles. Joseph Pietronov turned and leaned his left elbow on the bar, his eyes scanning the crowd. His gaze passed over Stiletto as the former CIA agent approached the bar, but the Russian's face registered no recognition. There was no reason he should know Stiletto's face, unless he'd been warned ahead of time that assassins directed by Kremlin proxies had targeted him.

By the time Stiletto reached the bar, Pietronov's drink was ready. The bartender tapped his shoulder, handed him the glass, and accepted Pietronov thanks and a tip. The bartender turned to Stiletto, who waved him off.

That caught Pietronov's attention. He frowned at Scott. "Not drinking?"

"No, Mr. Pietronov," Stiletto said.

"I don't believe we've met."

"We haven't, although you might recognize my name from cable traffic."

"You're a celebrity?"

"More infamous than famous," Stiletto said. "I'm Stiletto. *Scott* Stiletto."

Pietronov covered his reaction with a swallow of his drink. He lowered the glass. His face looked grim. "Yes, I know who you are, Mr. Stiletto."

"Are you aware your people, or people hired by your people, tried to kill me yesterday?"

"I've heard no such thing."

"Of course not. Check the news. You'll see it."

"Why are you here?"

"Because your bosses, by now, should have received word that the contract on my life is to be cancelled immediately. I'm working for The Trust now. You mess with them and you're going to pay."

"I'm aware of The Trust."

"You're also probably aware that when I escaped Moscow a few months ago, I had in my possession certain files. Files that detailed how the Kremlin uses Russian Mafia groups around the world for assassination and other dirty tricks."

"That I am not aware of."

"Your boss will know all about them. You're going to tell your boss, either first thing tomorrow or before the night is over, that I am still in possession of those files."

"I see."

"Moscow seems to think the opposite."

"Yet you've not released them already. Why is that?"

"Because I thought we could settle this, you know, like gentleman, over a drink, at a fancy embassy party." Stiletto smiled. "There's no need to upset world diplomacy over a little beef between me and your government."

Pietronov did not smile. "I will deliver your message. Is that all?"

Stiletto thought for a moment. There were plenty of other thoughts he could share with Pietronov, but they'd be the words of a man angry at the loss of friends in Moscow the night he escaped. He wanted to tell Pietronov that the days of the current leadership in the Kremlin were numbered. But he decided that he'd be wasting his time. Nothing ever changed in Russia. The instability of the nation, and the effort to hide such conditions, was as predictable as the sunrise.

"Tell your boss I'm done looking over my shoulder. Okay?"

"Message received, Mr. Stiletto. Please. Enjoy the rest of the party."

"I will," Stiletto said. And he meant it.

"That didn't take long," Beth said as Stiletto rejoined her. "Why am I here again?"

He took her hand. "Let's dance and I'll explain."

They hit the floor, the band playing a slow tune that allowed them to stand close and move slowly. Stiletto kept his voice low as he explained the conversation.

"How do you feel?"

"Ten times better than when I got here."

"Is that what the boss had in mind?"

"Oh, sure," Stiletto said, leading her into a turn. "I haven't been myself for months. There's now a weight gone from my shoulders. Tonight, I got my own back."

CHAPTER SIX

Scott looked up from his breakfast. He'd selected an omelet, full of diced ham and peppers, with a side of hash browns and a pot of tea. He smiled at Number One as the old man eased into a chair beside him.

"You look good, Mr. Stiletto."

"I feel good, sir," Stiletto said.

"Do you understand why I sent you to that party?"

"Yes. I think you're a genius."

"You're starting fresh. Congratulations. Most deserved."

"I think I could have avoided a lot of problems if I'd signed with you in the beginning."

"You made the best decision you could at the time," Number One said. "It was a noble decision, and you should not be ashamed of it."

"I'm not. Mostly."

"Have you told your handler in Paris of your decision?"

Number One referred to Suzi Weber, a former CIA

agent herself, confined to a wheel chair after an insurgent bombing in Iraq. She'd left the Agency to start her own service of brokering contracts to freelancers and taking a cut.

"Suzi's aware," Stiletto said. "She'll be available if I ever need help with something, but otherwise, yeah, we're done."

"Mr. Fleming will be expecting you in his office after you finish your meal. I'm heading back to Zurich and our hub there."

"Thank you for everything you've done."

"I should be thanking *you*, Mr. Stiletto. You will be an asset to this organization."

"I appreciate your confidence."

Number One rose. Stiletto stood as well, and shook the old man's hand. He didn't sit again until Number One had exited the cafeteria.

Stiletto met General Ike in his office, who said it was time for a tour of the lower levels. Stiletto followed Ike Fleming down a hallway to an elevator with nervous anticipation in his gut. He couldn't wait to see the engine that ran The Trust and its operations.

The elevator doors rumbled open on a large command center, the forward walls covered with large screens displaying various nuggets of information, a crew of 15 people manning work stations. Scott looked at the monitors, noting live-stream video from one part of the world, and a digitized map on another monitor.

"We have operatives in Oman right now," Fleming said. "Large operations against a terrorist cell there."

The walls were bright white, as were the lights, the work stations arranged in clusters of four, with staffers communicating quickly while they logged information into their computers.

Stiletto wasn't sure if the facility lived up to Beth's "state of the art" claims, but it was impressive. Fleming showed Stiletto the rest of the facility, the usual break rooms and meeting rooms, and explained how vents from above pulled fresh air to the underground "bunker", as he called it.

"This is where your support will come from when you're in the field," Fleming explained as they continued to watch the activity. "You'll have a control on this end, who can relay whatever messages you need to send to me, and chances are, most of the time, you'll have eyes in the sky watching you too."

Stiletto watched the overhead view of the Oman team on one of the large monitors as they prepared to breach the door of a building. The crew was in full kit—body armor, weapons—but Stiletto knew better than to ask who they were engaging. Such information was probably need-to-know only to those involved.

Back in Fleming's office, the General rotated the computer monitor on his desk to Scott could see it better.

Using a keyboard, Fleming called up a series of pictures.

"Now, your turn," Fleming said. "Ready to get back into action?"

"Try and stop me."

"As I've mentioned, we're involved in an anti-drug operation on Colombia against the Noguera Cartel. Your part of the effort starts in Boston."

Stiletto scooted closer to see the pictures on the monitor better. "Who are we looking at?"

"Giles Flynn. He's the top dog of the Boston Mafia. For now."

"Uh-huh."

"If there's anything worse than cancer, these guys are it."

Giles Flynn looked older than the 73 years the General claimed he was. His face showed a lot of miles.

"Drugs, prostitution, gambling, loan-sharking. Several murders every year, most unsolved."

"The Boston Mob has always been brutal," Stiletto agreed. "It was the only way to keep the Italians from entering their territory."

"Sometimes it even worked," the General said. He showed Stiletto pictures of the Flynn Mob on his desktop computer, Flynn the leader; Donald Reeves, the first lieutenant; and Tyrell Drummond, the most cold-blooded killer to ever populate the Boston syndicate, according to reports.

"They're working with the Colombian cartel," the

General said. "One of our goals at CIA was to find out how the Colombians approached Flynn. There's a go-between, we believe an American, working with the cartels to set up alliances here in the US. We have no idea who this person is, but he's believed to be responsible for setting up more than a dozen connections for cartels."

"Are these connections helping the cartels get drugs into the US?"

"Very much so. The US interests are making arrangements to bring drugs in, so the cartels have ceased their own efforts, and we're falling behind. The DEA and Justice Department like to tell the public we're stopping the flow of illegal narcotics, but this new situation is reversing that effort."

"What about informants in the cartels?"

"They've come up dry. Everything is arranged on the US side, and the cartels simply transport contraband to a staging point, where it's collected and taken across the border. These staging points are decided only hours before a shipment, which means our informants have not been able to learn them ahead of time."

"If we catch this go-between," Stiletto said, "we can close down more than one of these alliances, and leave the cartels starving for US access once again?"

"Exactly."

"You want me to ask Flynn the guy's name?"

Fleming laughed a little. "I see your sense of humor is intact." His smile faded. "No. You're going to terminate

Flynn. And his two subordinates. You are going to create a vacuum the Colombians will be desperate to fill."

"And the Colombians will reach out to their go-be-tween again," Stiletto said, "for the next connection."

"And this time, we'll be ready."

"Point me in the right direction, sir."

CHAPTER SEVEN

Boston, Mass.

Giles Flynn, top dog of the Irish mob in Boston, wasn't as young as he once was. But he could still kick a rock to the moon when required.

Like now.

There was a man, on his knees, in the center of the office floor. He'd been forced to his knees after a punch in the gut by the big man standing beside him. Flynn stepped away from his desk and kicked the man in the stomach as hard as he could.

Breath left the man and a painful yell escaped his lips as he collapsed onto the carpet, trying to suck air, his beaten body already in bad shape.

Flynn looked at the big man.

Donald Reeves waited patiently for Flynn to say something, but the boss was breathing hard through his nose, air hissing through his nostrils, his eyes hot with anger.

"I don't like rats who talk to the cops," Flynn said.

"I agree," Reeves told him. "The question is, how much damage has he done, and what do we do with him?"

Flynn glanced at the prostrate man on the floor. He was still whimpering, trying to get his breath back.

Flynn's office was at the top of a popular Boston night club called the Flynn Club. Posters of various local bands, all of whom having played on the Flynn Club stage in the past, covered the walls. Flynn wasn't a reader; no book cases, not even for show. The club was a legitimate operation, on the surface, but used mostly as a way for Giles Flynn to prove he had means of making a living, and launder money.

The man on the floor, Bill Millar, was part of Flynn's street crew. After several of his men were arrested by the Feds, Flynn initiated a hunt for the rat who tipped off the cops. Reeves, his number two, came up with Millar.

And now Millar was living on borrowed time.

"Where's Tyrell?" Flynn said.

"Probably out skinning a cat."

"Throw this piece of crap in the trunk of your car, go find that freakshow Tyrell, and do something permanent to this ... *thing*. I don't want to see this rat again."

Flynn kicked Millar in the ribs, his foot landing with a heavy thud that earned another cry from the man on the floor.

Scott Stiletto watched a sweaty man dig his own grave.

Stiletto lay flat on cold dirt with a blanket of night sky above him, peering through a rifle scope.

The sweaty man was Bill Millar, and he'd been taken 90 minutes outside Boston to a wooded area where nobody would hear or witness his murder.

Two other men stood above Millar as he dug the grave deeper, sinking the shovel into the earth, wiping his forehead with the wet sleeves of his shirt. Donald Reeves and Tyrell Drummond. Reeves would be the man in charge on the chilly night; Tyrell was like a wiener dog, always at his boss's heels.

Stiletto adjusted his scope to zero in on Reeves. The tank of a man had less hair than the surveillance pictures at headquarters had shown, and more lines on his face. His big nose sat between small eyes. He was still number two on the Flynn pecking order. He should have moved up years ago, but Flynn insisted of remaining upright despite his advanced age.

Tyrell Drummond was one of the fiercest killers walking the streets. Had he not been under the thumb of Giles Flynn, Drummond would have caused chaos in whichever city he chose, the kind of killer who'd need to fill a basement with several freezers to store collected body parts.

The two mob thugs taunted Millar now and then as Millar continued shoveling dirt, the pile beside his final resting place growing higher by the moment.

Stiletto lay behind the latest in U.S. Army sniper technology, a modified Heckler & Koch G28 rifle chambering the man-shredding .308 NATO cartridge. Magazine fed, with a bipod under the barrel, Stiletto had perfect cover of the killing zone ahead of him.

Millar jammed his shovel into the mud and leaned against the handle, gasping for breath.

Reeves said, "I think it's deep enough." He reached under his coat for a revolver. The Dan Wesson Model 44 flashed in the moonlight. It was an old gun. It's five-inch barrel had sent many a slug into rats like Millar, and maybe even a cop who refused to take a bribe.

Millar spun to face Reeves, looking up from the deep hole in the ground. For the first time, Stiletto had a good look at the man's face. His face was covered with bloody welts. Whatever had happened to Millar prior to digging the hole in the ground had been brutal indeed. And typical of the Boston mob.

"Wait! I told you it wasn't me! How can I prove it to you?"

Reeves fired once. Flame flashed from the .44 Magnum. The bullet split Millar's head like a watermelon dropped off a roof. As a piece went to the left, another to the right, along with pieces of brain and skull, Millar's body fell into the hole, and the handle of the shovel disappeared as it fell over on top of him.

"How we going to fill the hole?" Drummond said after the echo of the shot faded.

Reeves put his gun away.

"I should have asked him to hand me the shovel first."

"I'm not going in there."

"The hell you aren't, Tyrell. Get me that shovel."

"I don't want to get muddy."

"You're gonna get *bloody* if you don't do what I tell you, Tyrell."

Stiletto muttered to himself, "Idiots," as he took up slack on the trigger.

The H&K kicked against his shoulder and whatever Tyrell Drummond was going to say in response as he opened his mouth vanished in the mist of crimson that spat from either end of his neck. As his body fell back, Reeves recoiling with a scream, raising his arms to block the blood spatter, Stiletto fired again. The .308 slug went through the space between Reeves' raised arms, and smacked solidly into Tyrell Drummond's chest. The Mafiosi hit the ground with a thud.

Reeves shuffled back, almost falling into the hole, but managed to keep his balance. Stiletto fired again. Reeves' left kneecap popped loud enough to be heard as far as Wrigley, and as he landed in the dirt, yelling at the top of his lungs, Stiletto set the H&K rifle aside and stood. He started forward. Caked mud fell from his outfit of black jeans and a black sweater; the dirt that remained attached to the fabric of his clothes didn't distract him. He reached for the custom-built Colt Combat Government M1911-style .45 autoloader on his hip.

Reeves' cries became louder as Stiletto approached.

Finally, Scott stopped beside Reeves and said, "Hey."

Reeves snapped fearful eyes to Stiletto's. Stiletto had not covered his face with combat cosmetics. He wanted Reeves to see him. And he did.

Reeves let out a curse, his pain seemingly forgotten. He cursed again as Stiletto reached into a pocket in Reeves' jacket and plucked out his cell phone. Stiletto aimed the cell at Reeves and started recording video. "I'm going to send a video of me murdering you to your boss, Donald."

"No way! No way!"

"Total way."

Stiletto fired one shot from the .45. The hard-nosed slug punched through Reeves' left eye, snapping his head back, a short scream choking off as his body flopped once and lay still.

Stiletto kept the video aimed at the body a moment, then panned over to where Drummond lay, and finally settled on Millar in the hole.

"Hi, Giles," Stiletto said, panning back to the other bodies again. "I suppose telling you your guys aren't coming back isn't necessary, right?"

He let out a laugh, waited a moment, and pressed the stop button. He found Flynn's phone number in Reeves' list of contacts, and sent the video attached to a blank text. Dropping the cell on the ground, Stiletto split it into pieces with another blast from the .45.

Retracing his steps, Stiletto collected the Heckler & Koch G28 sniper rifle and found his way through the dark back to his SUV.

He felt nothing as he drove away. He hadn't killed any real people. He, more accurately, delivered long over-due justice to victims unknown to him, but victims nonetheless. As always, such people needed a champion. Stiletto had the abilities required for such a task; he was happy to oblige, because somebody had to, so why not him?

And he wasn't finished yet.

CHAPTER EIGHT

"How do I know we're even safe here?" Giles Flynn demanded. "How many bugs did you find?"

"Two," said Leon Nash. He produced the listening devices from a pocket of his slacks and tossed them on the boss's desk.

Nash stood about two inches taller than his elderly boss, and tried to keep cool while Flynn huffed and puffed while refusing to explain the current situation.

Leon Nash was Flynn's top assassin, the man called when brutes like Reeves and Drummond were the wrong men for a hit. But now Reeves was dead, along with his little buddy Tyrell, and Flynn suddenly had a bigger problem than a traitor to deal with.

"This isn't the Feds," Nash said, opening with an obvious statement that might break Flynn's zipped lips.

Flynn said, "You're learning."

Nash pressed his lips together to bite back a snarky reply. The boss wouldn't have appreciated the first response that came to mind.

They were in the upper office of the Flynn Club, and Nash couldn't believe Flynn had the gall to name the place after himself. It was a careless lapse. A middle-finger to the cops and everybody else who knew who Giles Flynn really was. Not the choice he'd have made.

Nash stood while Flynn sat behind a cluttered desk, the papers and notepads full of day-to-day club business. The charade was as thin as a worn bedsheet, to Nash, but the boss insisted on trying to keep up the façade. It was the way the game was played.

"You saw the video?" Flynn said.

"I saw the video," Nash said. "It was interesting."

"That's all you got? Two of our guys dead, one of whom was my best friend for *years*, and you think it's *interesting*?"

"My first thought was somebody trying to rescue Millar."

"Nope."

"The Italians? They aren't too happy we got the deal with the Colombians and they didn't."

Flynn waved that off. "Not the Italians."

Flynn's barrel chest sank a little. He was a big man still, but his age was undeniable. He was an old hawk surrounded by young bucks full of piss and vinegar who thought they should run the big show.

"One of our own people making a play?" Nash said.

"None of that," Flynn said. "It's a nightmare, plain and simple."

"A nightmare."

"I need you to find this nightmare and snuff it out."

Nash didn't stifle a chuckle. "Based on what?"

"Based on it's your job, Nash!"

There was no sense in pushing the old man. The deal with the Colombians to secure East Coast distribution of their cocaine had been tough, and took a lot out of him. What he needed was rest, some catch-up time, but now this new problem had developed. Nash didn't have to understand, he simply had to deal with the problem. And first he had to deal with the fact that he had nothing to go on, which made dealing with the problem that much harder. The best way to track down Mr. Nightmare might be to babysit Flynn since he would obviously be on the target list.

Somehow, he didn't think Flynn would agree to that idea.

"I'll get with the guys and start making some moves," Nash said.

"I want this man dead."

"You want him dead, got it."

"I want him so dead," Flynn said, raising his voice, "that he makes disco look like it's making a comeback!"

Nash chuckled, turning, heading for the office door. "I don't think I can make him any deader."

"You keep me updated," Flynn said to Nash's back.

"Uh-huh."

Nash shut the door behind him.

Stiletto removed the earbud as soon as he heard the door close. He sat in his SUV, parked curbside a block away from the Flynn Club. He laughed. Nash had received a tall order indeed.

He didn't know Leon Nash except through the dossier provided by headquarters, and then only his picture and background. A quiet assassin. He liked to kill up close when possible, and make deaths look like an accident when he couldn't.

He liked fancy suits, and expensive things. Unlike other mobsters, he stayed with one woman, and she was never far from him. He was new to the Flynn outfit. But with Reeves and Drummond now out of the way, Nash would be Flynn's next security blanket.

With the assassin neutralized, Flynn would only have his second- and third-string crew members to rely on. Which meant Flynn's main defense would be the young bucks who might see an opportunity to put the old man in the ground, which he'd know, and freak out even more.

If Stiletto pressured him long enough, the old man would keel over on his own and save Stiletto a bullet.

But Stiletto didn't have that kind of time.

Nash had found the two bugs placed in the office by Stiletto prior to the first kills in the forest. Stiletto had meant for those bugs to be found. They were conventional listening devices used by the government against the mob all the time, and easily detectable with equipment which the smart gangster made sure to acquire.

What Nash hadn't found were the undetectable bugs, the kind developed by the gee-whiz geniuses at the Trust, the kind of bugs that worked via nanotechnology and didn't give off a conventional signal, so Nash could scan the room all day and never find them. Stiletto had made sure they were hidden in the last place Nash, or anybody else, might look.

He watched the street. He didn't know which car was Nash's, but he waited a few minutes before exiting the SUV. The club wasn't open for business yet, only a small set-up crew, a bartender, and two or three goons, along with Flynn, would be there right now. With Nash out of the way, the odds were more in Stiletto's favor.

He wore gray slacks, matching jacket, and a black silk shirt with black shoes. The .45 rode in shoulder leather under his left arm.

Stiletto walked casually up the block, looking perfectly natural among the other pedestrians going about their nighttime festivities, and crossed the street to where Flynn's sat on the corner. He pulled on the door. It was locked, of course. He knocked. No answer. He pounded hard with his right fist. He didn't have to wait long.

A bald goon in a suit opened the door.

Stiletto punched him in the mouth.

He flailed backward, legs shuffling to keep him from falling. The goon fell against the ball where he reached for a pint glass and, like a quarterback, chucked it at Stiletto.

As the glass closed the distance, Stiletto ducked. The glass crashed behind him. He kicked the door shut and rushed to the goon as he came at Stiletto with fists, yelling. Stiletto batted away the blows, and bashed the side of the goon's head with the .45.

The man dropped at his feet.

Stiletto had no time to admire his work. A flight of steps off to the right led to the upper office, and a gunman at the top was screaming for the boss to get to cover as he leveled a machine pistol over the bannister. Stiletto ducked and rolled as the burst of slugs stitched the floor where he'd been. He rolled under a table. Stiletto fired twice. The first slug whined off the rail and punching through the ceiling, pieces of sheetrock falling on the goon as the second slug detached his chin and plowed through the rest of his head. The goon tumbled down the stairs.

A shotgun action click-clacked behind him. Stiletto rolled, coming up on his back, knocking down a table to use for cover. The bartender with the scattergun fired. The buckshot shredded the table, Stiletto using his left arm to cover his face. Pieces of Formica pelted his arm and suit. Stiletto fired over the table, his shots only destroying bottles on the back wall. The bartender pumped another round into his shotgun, but Stiletto fired again. The .45 slug took the bartender down, his body falling back against the shelves behind him. More bottles broke, more liquor spilling.

Stiletto scanned for more threats, but only three wait staff remained, and they were huddled in corners with fear-filled eyes.

He had to hurry.

Scott raced up the steps, stepping over the dead goon halfway. He kicked open the office door and jumped back as a salvo of automatic fire tore chunks out of the doorway. The gunfire stopped. Stiletto dropped low. Giles Flynn stood in front of his desk with an ancient MP-40 machine pistol, and he was working the bolt to clear a misfeed. Stiletto started forward. Flynn threw the machine pistol. Stiletto stepped left and let it fly by. Flynn shuffled back until he tripped, falling on his rear end with a short cry, scooting back further until he bumped into the front of his desk.

Stiletto aimed the .45 at Flynn's big nose.

"Get my video?" he said.

"You coward! Shooting an old man!"

Flynn breathed deep. Beads of sweat dotted his fore-head. Stiletto's pulse raced. He was a vulture circling above road kill. His finger twitched on the trigger.

"Drop the gun, sport," a voice from behind said.

This time, Flynn smiled. He wiped his forehead and grunted as he got to his feet. "While you were playing footsie downstairs, I called Nash and told him to get back here."

Stiletto turned his head. Leon Nash stood in the doorway with the bartender's shotgun.

The .45 thudded onto the carpet.

"Take him for a ride, Nash," Flynn said. "I hear there's still a big hole somewhere out in Dover that might fit this guy."

"With pleasure, Mr. Flynn."

CHAPTER NINE

Leon Nash traded the shotgun for Stiletto's pistol and escorted him to the parking lot behind the club. A crew would come over and clean up and close the place for the night. Somebody would take care of the cops, too, and keep them from sniffing around. All in a night's work.

Nash opened the driver's door of a dark Cadillac. "Get in and drive."

"You're doing it wrong, Nash. I'm not supposed to give *myself* a ride."

"This only ends one way. Get in."

Stiletto drove as directed, taking the highway out of the city, heading, once again, for Dover, and the place where he'd left the three other bodies. His hands were tight on the wheel. He'd screwed up and the big fish was getting away.

"Shouldn't you be trying to make a deal?" Nash said.

"You mean talk my way out of this?"

Nash laughed a little. "Not so smart now, are you?"

"When I'm driving, my full concentration is on the road. It's the only safe way to drive."

"Come on, impress me."

"You want me to beg."

"Sure."

"Not while I'm driving. When we reach our destination, I'm sure I will come up with a way to outsmart you."

"This I can't wait to see."

Traffic opened a little. Stiletto sped up. He started weaving around cars. Stiletto pressed the accelerator some more.

"Hey, slow it down."

"I'm a spirited driver," Stiletto said.

"I said slow it down." Nash jabbed the .45 into Stiletto's side.

"You shoot me, we crash. If we crash, we both die."

"Not in this thing. It's a Cadillac."

"Do you know how many people die in traffic accidents every year? There oughta be a law."

"Slow down."

"Have I impressed you yet?"

Stiletto cut off a bus and the Cad went over a bump that jolted them both. Stiletto moved into the right lane, moved the car close to the guard wall on Nash's side of the car.

"Hey!"

Stiletto floored the pedal. The big car surged ahead.

"Hey!"

Stiletto grinned as he moved in and out of the right

lane, each time closer to the guard wall. Nash shifted in his seat.

"Stop!"

"Impressed?"

Stiletto moved into the middle lane, flashing by other cars.

"I told you—"

Nash never finished the sentence. Stiletto swung the wheel to the right. The rear quarter panel of the Caddy smashed into the guard wall and the car spun out, crashing once, twice, into the concrete divider before coming to a stop on the right shoulder and facing the wrong way.

Stiletto and Nash, both jolted and stunned from the tumble, stayed still a moment, then unbuckled their seatbelts at the same time. Stiletto was a little faster and launched himself at Nash. Nash struck Stiletto on the left cheek. Stiletto punched Nash in the neck. Nash choked, raising the .45 to use like a hammer. Stiletto blocked the blow, twisting the autoloader out of Nash's hand. The other man's fingers broke with audible snaps. Stiletto struck Nash with the gun. Nash, still trying to breathe, started to come at Stiletto again, and Stiletto shot him in the face. The .45 slug turned his nose into a black hole, pushing it out the back of his head to shatter the passenger window. Nash's body slid down the seat. His knees bumped into the glove box.

Smoke drifted from the muzzle of the .45. Stiletto couldn't help himself. He lifted the muzzle to his lips and blew the smoke away.

Stiletto steered the Cad back into traffic, going the

wrong way just long enough to get back onto the right side of the road and head once again for the city, and ditched the car on the highway and continued the journey on foot.

He made it back to where he'd left the SUV without incident.

He didn't want to sit too long, so he drove away from the club, and found a shopping center parking lot where he paused to catch his breath and check himself in the rearview mirror. Nash's blows had landed hard. Nothing Stiletto hadn't survived before, but they'd still hurt.

He slumped in the driver's seat. Flynn would be fortified at home before the night was over. With Nash gone, he'd only have his house security to defend him. Once he learned of Nash's death, he'd send some of the street crews to look for Stiletto. The force at the house might not change, but he wouldn't overload with gunners if he thought Stiletto was wounded somewhere and hiding like an injured dog.

But the rest of Stiletto's mission depended on Flynn being out of the picture. It was the only way to find out how the Colombians had achieved their foothold on the East Coast. The Colombians were the primary target, and Stiletto needed Flynn gone to expose them.

This was a set-back, not a defeat.

He started the SUV once again and headed for his safe-house, established earlier by other Trust agents, which served as his base of operations.

Time to regroup.

CHAPTER TEN

Giles Flynn had a sinking feeling in the pit of his stomach that told him his home was no longer safe.

The large two-story home sat on a hill, surrounded by thick forest, in Newton, Massachusetts, about a 30-minute drive from Boston. Flynn did not spend a lot of time at the Newton estate, as he referred to the property. His patch had been carved out of the forest so, from above, one saw a big hole in the sea of trees. His house was on one side of the hole, followed by a large open yard, with a swimming pool on the opposite end.

A detached garage sat to one side. Flynn's pride and joy, a small vineyard for his personal wine-making effort, grew off to the left of the property and was the first thing one saw when driving up the access off Dudley Road. A smaller structure, near the pool, housed the security force, and the troops maintained a 24-hour presence on the property.

Twenty-four gunners in total. Tonight, Flynn had them

all on the clock, in the house, outside, and patrolling the perimeter. Twenty-four experienced shooters, and Giles Flynn didn't think they would be enough to stop *one man* from wiping him out.

One man!

One!

He was sick about Leon Nash. Poor bastard never had a chance. Who was after him and how had he managed to survive a professional killer like Leon Nash? It made no sense.

Giles Flynn turned from the bulletproof sliding glass balcony door on the top floor of the house, and stared into the empty bedroom. His family was there, elsewhere in the house, and he found it impossible to sit still because one man was out there waiting to pop a bullet into Flynn's gut and the Boston Mafiosi had no idea why, what for, or who was responsible for the specter of death's visitation.

He turned back to the sliding glass doors, looking out into the dark night. Pitch black outside. The forest blocked out the lights of the surrounding area of Newton. He was isolated out here. Alone.

Twenty-four gunners.

Against one man. One man who had taken out three people, two of whom were Flynn's best friends, Donald and Tyrell, snuffed them out like somebody turning off a lamp.

Not that Flynn hadn't done the same thing to others in his time, but when it's *your* pals, it's totally different.

And a chill at the back of Flynn's neck told him that

one man was indeed on the property, right now, as he stood staring. They'd meet face-to-face soon.

Flynn left the room in a hurry.

Only one gunner with the four-man patrol wore night vision, as if he was the only one who could afford the headset, or the others didn't think they needed one.

Stiletto wore a night vision set of his own, and he watched the four men moving in a staggered formation through the forest, the point man with the goggles leading the way. The other three looked capable enough, all wearing street clothes and no uniforms. They moved like trained soldiers, holding their automatic rifles properly, maintaining a danger scan and moving slowly, not like sloppy mafia goons who were only handed a gun and told what to do. This team knew how to move over rough terrain, and if they were a sampling of the force Stiletto would meet at the Flynn estate, he might have made a mistake coming alone.

He wasn't totally alone, however. An earbud nestled in his right ear connected to home base via satellite, and he had an "overwatch" named Rose to tell him the lay of the land. There were other friends along as well, including a M-4 automatic rifle with an M320 40mm grenade launcher mounted under the barrel, and a selection of high-explosive, smoke, and buckshot grenades across his chest.

The Colt .45 rode on his hip, along with spare magazines for the pistol and rifle. He was dressed head-to-toe in black, with dark smears of makeup on his face for further camouflage, and itching to begin a fight that would end his mission in Boston and send him along to the next stage of taking down the Noguera Cartel.

Rose said in his ear, "Status, Sierra Two?"

The Trust used a code-name system based on a person's name. Since "Scott Stiletto" would be Sierra Sierra in the phonetic alphabet, he was Sierra Two.

"Bogies ahead," he said, whispering. He didn't need to talk loud for Rose to hear him.

He had not met the woman, but imagined her sitting in the underground complex at HQ, watching him on a high-resolution satellite camera.

"I see them too."

He'd followed Dudley Road halfway up the hill before abandoning his rental on the side of the road, and entering the forest on foot. Very carefully he'd made his way to his current position, where he lay flat on his belly with the night-vision goggles giving him his first look at the enemy.

He decided there was no better way to introduce himself than with a 40mm high-explosive calling card.

The M320 loaded via the barrel breaking outward to accept the cartridge like a breech-loading shotgun. The barrel was then closed, the weapon primed, and the projectile fired when ready. Stiletto already had a grenade in the breech. He used the rifle sights to pick where he wanted the grenade to land, and pulled the trigger. The M320 belched with a hollow thump, the HE projectile racing across the 25-yards to target.

Somebody in the group knew what the *thump* was, because he shouted for everybody to scatter seconds after the noise of the discharge filtered to their ears. But the four-man patrol wasn't fast enough. The grenade struck the ground in the middle of the group and exploded, the concussion blast and resulting ball of fire lighting up the forest for an instant. Stiletto kept his head down after firing. He didn't want to flash of the explosion to blind him through the night-vision goggles. When the blast settled, he looked up. There were some trees on fire, but more importantly, a bunch of ripped bodies littering the forest floor.

Scott ejected the spent grenade and fed a new one into the breech, then closed the barrel and started moving. He maintained a slow pace through the trees and brush. There was no need to rush. The enemy knew he was there now; it was best to let *them* come to *him*. Until he was ready for the final push into the mansion itself, and his, hopefully, final confrontation with Giles Flynn.

"What's out there? What's happening?"

Giles Flynn had to stop himself from yelling into the walkie-talkie. Yelling would get them nowhere. But his pulse was racing. That explosion could only mean one thing.

"That blast came from the forest south of the house,"

said the leader of the security force over the hand-held, on the ground floor of the house. "We're checking on it."

"He's here!" Flynn shouted, unable to contain his fright any longer. He jammed the walkie-talkie into the pocket of his slacks and took a deep breath. *Calm down. Now is not the time to show fear when the girls are counting on you.*

He started down a hallway, only to be met halfway by his middle-aged wife and their two 20-something daughters. In a flood of panicked talk, the women wanted to know what to do, and Flynn took command like the leader he knew he truly was. He accompanied the three women to the ground floor, telling them not to look at the hustling hulks of armed men taking up defensive positions around the lower level, where he had his "safe room", an armored box built into the basement of the house. Nothing short of a nuclear bomb could break through that box, and he didn't think his mysterious enemy had access to *that* kind of firepower.

Stiletto reached the tree line as the Flynn troopers outside the house scrambled for cover.

"Sierra Two, you're clear in back and side to side."

"Copy."

After the edge of the tree line, there was a large swimming pool and side house Stiletto figured was for the troops. Beyond the pool, an open area of grass prior to the big house. If the bad guys had trouble finding a place to hide, it wasn't a picnic for Scott, either. He had to find a way to cross that open chasm while dealing with more than one armed trooper.

He looked to the right. The thick forest wrapped around the property. If Scott could make his way around the perimeter while remaining concealed, he might breach the side of the house closest to the detached garage.

But first, some distraction for the ungodly.

Stiletto grabbed a smoke grenade from his bandoleer, popped open the breach of the M320, and replaced the high-explosive charge with the smoke grenade. He fired at the furthest group of Flynn troops, off to his left. He opened the breach again and popped a buckshot round into the M320. Upon detonation, the grenade would spew hundreds of steel balls in all directions, the projectiles guaranteed to hurt or destroy anything they came in contact with.

As a thick veil of smoke drifted across the yard, Stiletto fired the buckshot round. When it detonated, several wails of pain followed. Return fire crackled, but none of the rounds landed near Scott.

They were firing blind. Scott fired off another smoke, this one to his right, to further confuse the enemy, and began moving through the rough terrain, following the perimeter.

"Base," he said, "how does the house look?"

"Heat signatures inside, but otherwise everybody is out front."

"Copy."

CHAPTER ELEVEN

The safe room didn't protect the Flynn family from the rumbles of explosions outside that shook the walls.

"What's going on, Giles?"

Flynn had nothing to look at except the steel walls which surrounded them, the room lit by bright fluorescent lights, couches on either side of the walls. It wasn't a room meant for a long stay. It was a room meant to keep the family protected in an event such as they were suffering tonight: somebody on the property intent on murdering them.

But the walls communicated nothing, so Flynn turned to the woman who'd asked the question.

His wife, Barbara, might have had more lines on her face than she did when they first met, but she was still beautiful, and still a fireball, as she stood in front of their twin daughters who were their mother's spitting image.

"Tell me, Giles!"

"We're in trouble."

"That's it?"

"I don't know what else to tell you, babe. Somebody gunning for us."

"And you led us down here into this death trap?"

"We're safe here!" He stepped closer to her. She didn't back away. "I built this room to keep us safe!"

The twins, Maggie and Tammie, otherwise referred to as The Heartbreakers because of all the boys they burned through, or sometimes *the Blessing* (Maggie—the good girl) and *the Curse (*Tammie—the bad girl*)*, sat close together on one of the couches, watching him with wide eyes.

He hated the son of bitch outside even more now for making his little girls scared.

"We don't feel safe, Giles."

"We're surrounded by a steel box designed to withstand a bomb blast, Barbara. Nothing's getting through here."

"And if the security team fails?"

"Whoever this shooter is, he can't stay all night. He's woken up half the city by blowing up the yard, the cops will be on the way."

Barbara Flynn folded her arms and fumed at her husband.

Giles Flynn stared at her, fighting back a feeling of desperation. There was nothing he could say to calm her down. There was nothing he could say to reassure his daughters. More explosions boomed above them. The walls shook some more. Giles Flynn looked at the walls once again and hoped they'd indeed take the punishment.

The only connection he had to anybody upstairs was the intercom by the door. The captain of the guards would tell them when the house was clear of intruders.

But the longer they waited, the more Giles Flynn feared there would be nobody to tell them "all clear".

His "safe room" might turn into the family tomb.

Stiletto stopped beside a tree trunk, the soft dirt beneath his feet yielding to his weight. The Flynn troops were still hovering around the spot of the first grenade blast, searching the area, but only a few venturing into the forest itself. Stiletto shouldered the M-4 and began firing short bursts, the crackles of the automatic weapon loud and clear, the troops breaking for cover once again.

The green haze through the night vision goggles didn't have infrared capability, so the drifting smoke hindered him as well as them, but Stiletto caught a few in the open, the gunmen stopping short as bullets struck, as if they'd hit a wall, to tumble to the ground. Others flattened in the grass. Stiletto fired a longer burst at those still exposed, then shifted his aim to the tree line as troops searching through the foliage began to emerge.

The M320 belched again, the fireball of high-explosive ordnance taking down most of the gunners. Stiletto fired out the M-4's magazine, the action locking back, and reloaded on the run as he headed for the detached garage beside the house.

The outside force was pretty much decimated, though a few stragglers might recover their wits long enough to venture into the house. He worked his way around the garage, careful of any troops nearby, saw none, and crossed a paved walkway to the side of the house. He trusted Rose, but also couldn't turn off his own combat instincts.

Peeking in a window, he ducked back quickly upon seeing movement there. But the trooper didn't see him. He and others appeared to be heading for the front of the house. Stiletto worked his way around back. The back of the house ran up against the rear tree line, only a small amount of open space there. Not even a patio set up. The back didn't see any activity. Scott blasted the back doors open, crashing through in a shoulder roll. He immediately leaped to his feet and scanned for targets.

The wide room, shaped in a half-circle, was a lounge with windows looking out on the backside, and appeared to clean to be used regularly. Stiletto advanced forward, up a set of steps, to a walkway with polished tiled floor leading straight to the front door.

"Two hostiles coming your way, Sierra Two."

The gunmen appeared at the end of the walkway, investigating the shots from the rear. Stiletto pulled the trigger of the M-4 and set a salvo of rounds into both targets. The gunners twitched as slugs sliced through them, falling onto the tiles, another gunner running to their aid and slipping on the blood-wet tile. As his body hit the floor, Stiletto fired again, punching a string of rounds through his head and upper body which kept the man pinned with his buddies.

Stiletto moved to a corner as more troopers crashed through the front door, firing as they entered, Stiletto triggering a high-explosive grenade that touched off a fireball within the vestibule that scorched anything that moved. Scott ejected the spent grenade and added a buckshot. The second blast finished off whatever had survived the first.

His ears ringing from the blasts, Stiletto waited, the M-4 still at his shoulder. But nothing emerged from the carnage. He started forward again, scanning each room along the hallway, the kitchen, another sitting area with television, nothing out of the ordinary for the average American home, albeit the house was bigger than average, and contained a crew of armed gunners instead of a simple house alarm.

"I'm still seeing heat signatures, but it appears they're below the house."

Stiletto frowned. A basement hideout? "Copy, Base."

Scott turned down another hall and checked bedrooms, noting feminine details to two of the bedrooms. The master was empty; going back the way he came, he started down another hall, with a room at the end. A den, with obvious male touches, also empty.

Then Stiletto heard a voice.

"What's going on up there? Can anybody hear me?"

CHAPTER TWELVE

Giles Flynn pressed the Talk button again.

"Can anybody hear me?"

Barbara and the girls, huddled on the couch, sobbed quietly, and Giles Flynn wanted to tell them to suck it up and act like men. Yelling at his wife and daughters wasn't going to get them out of their predicament, however. He needed a status update from the top, and tried to hide the fact that his hands were shaking as he moved away from the intercom speaker.

The speaker blipped. Flynn's attention perked.

"Hey, Giles. How's it going?"

Flynn's blood ran cold. *That voice.* The voice of the man who'd sent a recording of Donald Reeves' execution. The man who almost killed him in his own club.

Flynn's wife and daughters froze, too, as Flynn slapped the Talk button and put his mouth close to the speaker.

"Who are you?"

"Come on up and we'll talk about it."

"We aren't talking. The second I see you I'm going to kill you!"

"I'll be waiting."

Giles Flynn pulled back from the intercom as if the button had burned him. He glanced at his family. The girls, sobbing on their mother's shoulders, weren't looking at him. Barbara's eyes pleaded for reassurance.

"You aren't going up there, Giles!"

"I don't know what else to do, Barbara!"

They had no way to call out. No choice but to wait until the shooter couldn't hang around any longer. How long would that take? The numbers were falling. Fast. The intruder had minutes. Maybe less. Yet he was still up there, apparently, waiting for Giles Flynn to emerge from hiding for a showdown.

There wasn't much time left.

Scott couldn't wait all night for Flynn to come out of the panic room, or whatever he called it. Scott slung his M-4 and opened the pouch on his left hip, taking out blocks of C-4 plastic explosive which he began planting around the house, activating the remote receivers on each block. Red lights flashed on the detonators, the bricks otherwise inert, ready for the electrical impulse from Stiletto's hand-held detonator that would set off the blasts and collapse the mansion like a house of cards.

Stiletto returned to the intercom and pressed the Talk

button.

"Giles."

A moment. Then: "What?"

"Come out."

"We're not going anywhere, hot shot. I don't know who you think you are—"

And Giles Flynn ranted a few minutes about how tough he was and how he owned Boston and would see Stiletto's ears in a jar for a trophy. Scott let the old man rant. And rant. Gangsters might not be good at much, but they were good at ranting. Giles Flynn ranted with the best.

When the blustering dialogue ended, Stiletto pressed the button again.

"Finished?"

Expletives in reply.

"Hey, listen, it's getting late," Stiletto said. "I've wired the house with C-4. I'm going to bring the walls down on you and your family unless you come out."

"You'll do it anyway!"

"Try me. My fight isn't with your family, Giles."

"I'd like to know why you're fighting *me*!"

"Blame the Colombians."

Silence. Stiletto hurried to reload the M-4 as he heard heavy movement below the floor. The basement. A door crashed. Stiletto moved in that direction, M-4 at the ready.

Despite the girls' protests, Giles Flynn exited the safe room, shutting the door tight, and started up the steps to the first level of the house. Slamming open the basement door, he stood in the hallway and froze at the sight before him.

A man dressed in black, holding an automatic weapon with a grenade launcher attached under the barrel.

Grenade launcher?

Who was this guy? The same man who had almost killed him in his own club, that's who. And this time there was nobody coming to his rescue.

"Here I am!" Flynn announced.

"Good bye, Giles."

The automatic rifle flashed flame and Giles Flynn felt his insides rip apart. He tried to remain standing, falling first against the left side wall, leaving a smear of red as he tumbled to the floor. He tried to call to his family, but a dark void enveloped him before he let the words out.

Stiletto watched Giles Flynn die, his final half-cry not penetrating to the basement where the intended recipients remained hidden.

Stiletto beat it out of there. Out the back, around the house, across the front yard where he ran unmolested. The stink of cordite and explosive residue filled the air. As Stiletto reached the tree line, he grabbed the remote detonator from his battle vest, and pressed the button. A series of muted booms, followed by the harsh shattering of windows as the explosive pressure sought release, filled the property.

He had no qualms about wiping out Flynn's family along with the crime boss. They were as guilty as him, even if they hadn't participated in crimes. They lived lavishly off the pain and suffering of others. To Stiletto, that marked them same as the old man. They had a chance to survive, if the safe room had been designed properly; then again, they might not.

Scott watched fire engulf the house. Then he turned and ran into the forest, putting that place behind him. Giles Flynn was dead. Mission accomplished.

"How's the road, Base?"

"You're clear. We've intercepted several 9-1-1 calls so the police haven't been alerted yet."

Stiletto grinned. The Trust was thorough indeed.

Now to watch the Colombians, and wait for their next move once they realized their East Coast connection was a burning corpse.

But Scott Stiletto didn't know the Flynn women, their fortitude, or how much he was wrong about them. They didn't simply live off their father's efforts, they were part of the organization, and very soon Scott's only regret would be that he had depended on bombs to finish the job instead of doing it up close and personal.

Very soon indeed.

CHAPTER THIRTEEN

Ocean City, Maryland

"No."

The client looked across the haze of cigar smoke at Edward Kasson as if he'd grown an antenna out of his forehead.

"What do you mean, no? This job will be good for you."

"Good? How?" Edward Kasson said. "Jack, I'm over 50. My knees hurt. My back hurts. I've been fighting other people's wars most of my life. I can't do it anymore."

"Are you retiring?"

"Did I say that? I said I can't lead a mercenary force in Africa or wherever you want to send me. No more. I can't. Simply cannot do it."

"What *are* you looking for?"

Kasson set down his cigar on the small table. He and the client, Jack Nolan, sat in the corner of a cigar lounge in Ocean City, Maryland. The place catered to locals, not tourists, and they nearly had the place to themselves. Two other smokers sat near the big screen wall-mounted television watching a superhero movie.

"Something soft," Kasson said.

"Good luck with that."

"Thanks for thinking of me."

"Ten million, Eddie. Ten million bucks. A couple of weeks' work."

"No."

"Then I'll call somebody younger." Nolan climbed off the high chair.

"My blessings," Kasson said, as Nolan walked away in a huff, leaving his cigar barely smoked in the table's center ashtray.

Kasson turned his attention to the movie on the big screen, but only watched absently. There was a time, not long ago, when he would have jumped at the chance of a ten-million-dollar payday and go play war in the desert. Or the jungle. Or even, for a decade when he was much younger, the inner cities of Southern California.

Edward Kasson had white hair that stuck up on top of his head, a face with more lines than he cared to admit, and, under his suit, a body with more scar tissue than actual flesh, despite the muscled frame and broad shoulders. He'd been a warrior all his life, from the Marines to the CIA to the underground world of mercenary forces fighting whatever enemy he was pointed at and cashing his pay appropriately. The physical punishment of war, and age, was catching up with him. His fighting days were over. His body told him that every morning when he tried to get out of bed and everything hurt, from head to toe and back again.

He'd called Ocean City home for the last ten years, owning a small beach house, overlooking the ocean, where he could sit on his deck, drink coffee, hurt all over, and ponder the rest of his life. He wasn't hurting financially, but a little more cushion in the account wouldn't hurt.

An hour later he finished the cigar and left the lounge for his favorite lunch spot on the beach, where he sat under the awning, enjoying the sounds of the surf, and ate a very good hamburger with everything on it.

By the time he reached his house, walking to keep his joints moving, there was somebody waiting for him on the front deck. A man in a loose shirt and shorts, wearing sunglasses, holding a beer in each hand. With a bright white smile, he held up the beers as Kasson approached.

"Where you been?"

Kasson sighed. Another potential client. Perry Ross. Much younger than Kasson, Ross had a similar background, but managed to keep himself on the side of the business where he could hire the mercenary crews, stay warm stateside or Europe, whatever the job called for, and let somebody else get hurt.

Kasson climbed the steps to the deck and took a beer

from Ross's left hand. He popped the top with a twist.

"Telling another client to get lost."

Ross laughed and they clinked bottles and sat down. The chairs were positioned in front of the living room window, the drapes blocking the view inside. Not that Kasson had anything fancy inside. His tastes were simple and leaned toward comfort rather than flash, which meant mismatched couches and chairs, but he wasn't trying to impress anyone.

"You might like what I have to offer," Ross said.

"Try me."

"I have an opportunity available for somebody who has connections for getting contraband into the United States."

"What kind of contraband?"

"You know."

"No, I don't know, Perry. I've had enough of the word games. Come out with it."

"Somebody's sure grumpy."

Kasson muted his response with a long drink of beer. The brew tasted good, but the crashing waves on the opposite side of the street in front of the house was much better. The air was tinged with a salty scent.

Ross said, "The job requires you to work with people south of the border."

"Where?"

"Far south. Colombia."

"Drugs again?"

"Yes, Eddie, drugs. Lots and lots of drugs. Lots and lots of *illegal* drugs, get it?"

"I understand."

"You'll be working with a cartel."

"Okay."

"Should be old hat for you, right?"

Kasson laughed and drank some more beer. When he was with the CIA, in his younger years, he'd been instrumental in running crack cocaine and other illicit narcotics into the United States for the purposes of funding the Agency's secret wars in Central America. He'd done a lot of that work in South Central Los Angeles, the one area of the operation that had leaked to the press and caused decades of controversy and weak-kneed Agency denials. Kasson was glad, as were many other CIA suits involved in the operation, that South Central was the only phase of the operation that the public knew about. There was a whole lot more they *didn't* know about. But Kasson knew all about it.

Yeah, he knew drugs. He knew "south of the border".

"I'm interested," Kasson said.

"The Colombians had a guy on the east coast that was helping them get stuff into the country," Ross said. "Somehow or other, that connection got wasted and isn't there anymore. Now they want somebody not as high-profile."

"What does that mean?"

"It was a mob guy in Boston," Ross said. "The deal came with heat they weren't expecting. Now they want somebody off the radar of federal law enforcement, get it?"

"Uh-huh." Kasson drank some beer.

"We'll meet with a lawyer who will facilitate the meeting between us and the Colombian representatives," Ross said.

"What do you mean, *we* and *us*, Perry?"

"I want a piece of this one."

Fair enough. "When?"

"I'll call you." Ross set his barely touched beer on the table and stood.

"You didn't finish your beer."

"Do the honors," Ross said, as he went down the deck steps to the driveway. Moments later, Kasson heard his car start and drive away.

Kasson finished his beer and then, because he had nothing else to do, finished Ross's, all the while watching the waves crash on the beach and enjoying the salty tinge to the fresh air.

CHAPTER FOURTEEN

Betsie Fleming turned off the burner and scooped scrambled eggs from pan to plate. Her husband, Isaac, already dressed in a suit and tie, sat at the breakfast table with a tablet computer in front of him. From what she remembered when he took his new job, a daily briefing, scrambled just like his eggs, was emailed to the tablet and decrypted when he opened the file. He sat quietly, drinking his coffee, and reading the information on the screen.

She knew better than to ask what he was reading as she set his plate in front of him. He thanked her, clearing the screen, and setting the tablet aside as he picked up salt and pepper and seasoned his eggs. She served herself, and they sat and ate, picking at a stack of toast in the center of the table.

It was their morning routine. And as long as Betsie Fleming could remember, her husband was always reading work information received overnight during breakfast. He could have retired after leaving CIA. They were properly set up financially, there was no need for him to keep working, but within Isaac Fleming existed a drive that Betsie didn't quite understand. He wasn't *working*; he was serving.

Some things never changed.

Ike Fleming certainly wished he could share what he was reading with Betsie. But rules were rules. At least she understood. He'd worked with many fellows at CIA who were now divorced because their wives didn't understand why they couldn't talk about work, among other things.

But now it was breakfast time, and he and Betsie had their usual morning chat. She was retired, and had a busy day planned with her quilting club. The next day was book club, the day after that was wine club, and then, and then. . .

Fleming joked that his wife had more to occupy her attention now that she was retired than when she taught high school.

As they talked, the contents of the morning report bounced around Fleming's mind. It was all about Stiletto's efforts in Boston.

He was pleased with the report, although he knew the Flynn syndicate's destruction was temporary. They would ultimately rebuild, but that wasn't Fleming's problem. Let the FBI handle that. The door was now open for the Colombian cartel to find a new connection in the United

States, and Fleming hoped, this time, they'd spot the US representative who had brokered the deal with Flynn.

After breakfast, Fleming cleared the table, grabbed his tablet and briefcase, kissed Betsie good-bye, and left the house for Trust HQ.

"Sit down, Scott."

Stiletto took the chair in front of the big boss.

"You look a little rough," Fleming said.

"Tree branches are my greatest enemy," Stiletto said.

"Everybody's happy with the results," the General said.

"Survivors?"

"Flynn's family. Wife and two daughters."

"I thought they might."

"Firefighters found them in the basement vault, so to speak. Flynn's little panic room was built to withstand a nuclear blast."

"Who's keeping tabs on them while we move on?"

"The FBI. They'll be very interested in who attempts to take Flynn's place. The whole organization is in a state of chaos right now, but they're behaving. Once they bury Giles Flynn, you get bet more bodies will start to drop as the crew fights over the big chair."

"But that's not what we're going to talk about today."

"No." Fleming eased back in his chair, crossing his legs. "Time for the next leg. Are you ready?"

"My trigger finger is itching."

"Good. Because we have a big, fat target for you."

General Ike leaned forward to rotate his desktop computer monitor to Stiletto could have a better view. He said, "Time to learn more about the Noguera Cartel."

CHAPTER FIFETEEN

General Ike brought a wireless keyboard to the desktop and tapped a few keys.

"They run drugs, kidnap people, including American tourists, for ransom, generally bad sorts straight out of central casting without a hint of irony," Fleming said. A face appeared on the monitor. A young man with a mustache and dark hair.

"Amadis Noguera is a young buck, around 40, but he took down his father and assumed leadership of the cartel," the General said.

"How?"

"Shot his old man while he was on the toilet."

"Fascinating," Stiletto said. He examined the young man's facial features. High cheekbones, sharp jaw, the boring stuff. Noguera had dark eyes, but that's not what caught Scott's attention. What he noticed more than anything else was a cheek tattoo of what looked like a double-bladed dagger. "Is that what I think it is?"

"Yup," Fleming said. "Amadis used such a weapon on the first man he killed, an informant, of course. He wants everybody to know he's not afraid to get up close and cut a man's guts out."

Stiletto sat back and shook his head. "Can't central casting find us a bad guy who likes cats?"

The General only offered a sad shake of his head, adding, "That's a different book."

Stiletto figured he knew where the boss was going next. "Noguera is the one sending a delegation to the go-between we're eager to capture?"

"Yes."

"When's the delegation arrive?"

"We know he's sending two representatives to meet with a new connection in the US," the General said.

"Not the go-between."

"No."

"Instead it's the guys who want to take Flynn's place?"

"Yes."

"What do you want me to do?"

"We want the meeting to happen, the parties to separate. Follow the people they meet. More than likely, they will communicate with the go-between, and then we'll have him."

"Solo effort, or are we putting a band together?" Stiletto said.

"You'll be working with Beth Carrington, and two other agents named Greg Foster and Mitch Lang. Greg and Mitch are as good as Beth."

"When and where?"

"New York City. Manhattan Mall. We have a little more than twenty-four hours to prep."

Stiletto left his chair. "We better stop talking then, sir."

Fleming said, "Check in with the technical people downstairs. They'll have some toys for you."

"Some assembly required?" Stiletto said as he headed for the door.

"Probably. I told them to include batteries."

"Good thinking, sir."

Stiletto pulled the office door shut behind him.

New York City

Edward Kasson picked up a stray piece of greasy pepperoni from where it fell on his paper plate and popped it into his mouth. It wasn't the first time he'd enjoyed genuine New York-style pizza prior to a meet, but it was his first time doing both in the busy food court of the somewhat claustrophobic Manhattan Mall.

The mall was two stories of stores packed one atop the other, a seemingly narrow space, and Kasson didn't like it one bit. If things turned sour during the meeting, he needed space to run. The mall didn't offer space. It offered a lot of obstacles, human and otherwise, to avoid while running for an exit. Luckily, there were plenty of exits, plenty of vehicular traffic on the street outside, and a subway adjacent.

Across the small table, Perry Ross ate his pizza with a knife and fork and a napkin jammed in his collar. Ross always found a way to keep his hands clean, and worked hard at it. His nails were neatly trimmed, Kasson noticed. There was no fingernail under which dirt or any sign of real work could hide.

Kasson understood Perry wanted a piece of the action, but he didn't like the idea. Kasson worked best with other warriors who knew how to fight, and looked out for each other when the bullets were flying. He wasn't sure Ross possessed the same fortitude. The drug business was ugly. Could Ross handle that?

Kasson would feel better if Ross knew his place. As a subordinate to *him*.

And there was only one way to force him into that position. Teach him who's boss.

"Who's the mastermind behind this meeting?" Kasson said.

"I told you not to ask."

"You know me better than that. I'm going to ask."

Kasson didn't worry about speaking loudly. There was so much noise in the food court that nobody could tell one jumble of voices over another.

Ross jammed his fork into a cheesy bite and chewed without taking his eyes off Kasson.

Kasson only grinned. Ross was trying to intimidate him

into being second fiddle. *He* was in charge. This meeting was *his* idea. But Kasson wasn't having it. Kasson had faced death on too many occasions to be intimidated by a man who had a monthly manicure/pedicure appointment.

"You know who we're meeting, Eddie."

"I know who we're meeting. I want to know who arranged the meeting."

"You'll see him after we're done."

"Tell me his name."

"Why?"

"Because I really don't like former spooks who think everything is need-to-know. Sound familiar?"

"I don't get it, Eddie. You've never asked these many questions before."

"Because usually you hire me to take care of business and stay out of the way. This time, you're in my way."

Ross swallowed and drank some water. If he was surprised that Kasson knew of his previous experience at the Central Intelligence Agency, he gave no sign.

"He's a lawyer," Ross finally said.

Kasson smiled.

"He does mostly drug cases, and he has an inside guy at DEA who funnels information to him."

"What kind of information?"

"Not relevant to us."

"Sure it is," Kasson said.

Ross sighed. "Information that keeps him valuable to the cartels, get it?" he said. "They trust him, so he helps out on coordinating meetings like this in the US."

Kasson nodded and ate some more. It was enough for now. He'd managed to pry out of Ross what Ross didn't want to divulge, and that made Kasson the top dog. Ross could say all he wanted about being in charge, but Kasson had reduced his role by not letting the younger man keep his lips zipped.

Finally, Kasson asked another question that was burning a hole in the back of his mind.

"How in the world," he said, "can you eat pizza with a knife and fork?"

Ross shrugged. "I was posted in London for a few years."

"You're not in London anymore, Perry."

"Yeah, but this is so much better than eating like a Neanderthal," Ross said.

Kasson shook his head and took a big bite. Through a mouthful of cheese, pepperoni and crust, he said, "You look like a prissy idiot."

Ross laughed. "Remember who you're talking to. I'm writing your checks on this job."

"Remember I've killed maybe one hundred men," Kasson said, "and that total only covers the last five years. Want to know how many more there are?"

Ross blanched.

Now it was Kasson's turn to laugh.

CHAPTER SIXTEEN

No eye in the sky this time but Stiletto was grateful for a full team.

"Where are you, Sierra Two?"

The voice was Beth Carrington's, codenamed Bravo Charlie, low in Stiletto's right ear, the sat-linked earbud nestled comfortably. All Scott needed to do was talk normally, and Beth and the other two Trust agents at the Manhattan Mall would hear him.

"Just got into the elevator."

"We have eyes on target. They haven't met anybody yet."

"Save a slice of pizza for me. Extra pepperoni."

"Copy that."

The channel went quiet, but Stiletto knew they were still listening should he need to shout an alarm. If he needed help, well, he was on his own, but that wasn't a big deal. The .45 rode under his jacket. If he needed more than that, he was out of luck. Based on what happened at the hotel in Washington, DC, Scott was happy to at least be alone in the elevator.

Beth and the other two agents, Greg "Golf Foxtrot" Foster and Mitch "Michael Lima" Lang, were covering the representatives of the Colombian cartel, while Stiletto was going to search their hotel room for any information that might aid their investigation. He had a tote bag in the left pocket of his jacket, one that could be stuffed into a small pouch for carrying and open up to full size. Not one of the gadgets created by the gee whiz people at Trust HQ, but cool enough.

Stiletto did have one gadget from the Trust technical specialists, however. It was a hotel room key card programmed to match the ones issued at the Hotel Pennsylvania, conveniently located almost adjacent the Manhattan Mall. No need to stay somewhere fancy for a quick meeting, as rates at the Pennsylvania were quite reasonable with free breakfast for lodgers. Stiletto almost felt sorry he might have to rough up a room a little. He didn't want the cost of repairs to put a dent in the Svenhard's Bear Claw budget.

Beth Carrington, Greg Foster and Mitch Lang had a better toy, a directional microphone/4k camera hidden in a specially-designed purse for Beth to point at the cartel players during their meeting. He wouldn't be there to witness the actual meet, but Stiletto was sure they'd get a lot out of the recording once the conversation took place.

The elevator opened on the sixth floor and Stiletto

started down the quiet hallway, his footsteps silent on the carpet, checking the key card once more for the room number. 608. He didn't notice any of the hallway decorations. It was a hotel hallway, same as all the other he'd ever visited, and he was more interested in an ambush than admiring the wainscoting.

Trust operatives in Colombia had been able to trail the Noguera cartel representatives and hand them off to a surveillance team in the US, but if those same operatives south of the border hadn't been able to determine the identity of the go-between, the man's identity was a secret better kept than any others Stiletto had ever come across.

Beth's voice sounded in his ear. "We got a meeting, Sierra Two."

"Who are they talking to?"

"Two white males, one in his fifties, the other younger. They don't ring any bells in the mental mug file."

"Copy. Almost at the Colombians' room."

"Lima is getting video from the food court."

"Copy. I'm at the room."

Beth didn't reply. Stiletto slipped the counterfeit key card into the automatic lock and pulled it out. The indicator light on the lock switched from red to green followed by a soft *click* and Stiletto turned the knob.

For a city with a predominately gray color on the outside, interior designers in New York City seemed to go for lighter colors on the inside, and the Hotel Pennsylvania was no exception. The room Stiletto stepped into, letting the door shut behind him, was heavy on beige from wallpaper to drapes with the carpet the only dark color. Even the faux-wooden headboards at each bed had a light shading.

The entryway contained the usual closet on the right and bathroom on the left. Around the corner, the sleeping/ work area. The twin beds faced the flat-screen television on the forward wall. Windows looked out on the street below and buildings across the way. The work table be-side the bed was small, and cluttered with room service menus, and assorted sheets of paper advertising local sights organized in a plastic holder.

Stiletto only paid attention to the beds. Two suitcases were neatly packed on top of each bed, but on the bed nearest the door a third bag, this one pink, stood out like a fat lip.

The packed luggage meant the cartel reps weren't planning on staying once they completed their task. They had arrived the night before, slept, and planned to leave as soon as their chat was over. But there were three bags, not two, and the color of the third bag sounded an alert in Stiletto's mind.

Scott said, "Bravo Charlie?"

"Yes."

"How many cartel reps?"

"Two."

"Male and female?"

"Both male."

"Well, they brought three bags."

"So?"

"One of them is pink and sparkly."

"Lima, Foxtrot, any other players on scene?"

"Negative, Bravo," said Foster.

"I don't see anybody hanging back," replied Lang.

Beth said: "Hurry, Sierra, it looks like they're almost done. Smiles and handshakes."

Stiletto acknowledged and started with the closest suitcase. There was nowhere else to look but the luggage. The hotel room was already immaculate, having been scrubbed cleaned by the staff, and anything of value out of view. The first suitcase contained men's clothes and a tablet computer in a side pocket. Stiletto took out his own tote, shook it to full size, and dropped the tablet inside.

The next bag, the pink one, with the sparkly swirl on either side, contained women's clothing and a makeup kit.

The third suitcase, more men's items, revealed another tablet that Stiletto took possession of. The inner pocket also contained sheets of hotel stationary, torn from a pad, with various scribbles on them. Stiletto took the bundle and zipped the bag.

"They're leaving," Beth said.

"I'm on 'em," Mitch Lang said. "Sierra Two, I'll tell you when they reach the hotel."

"Did they pick up a lady friend?"

"Still no sign of a female."

"I'm getting out of here," Stiletto said.

He turned and took two steps toward the room.

The lock clicked and the door swung inward.

A woman stepped in, a statuesque Latina with olive skin, wearing a blouse with gray slacks, flat shoes, gold hoop earrings. She stopped short when her dark eyes landed on Scott's.

"Guys," Stiletto said, "I found the lady."

The woman shut the door, frowning at Scott. She dropped her purse on the floor and didn't waste time saying hello. Instead, she cracked her knuckles and launched at Stiletto with a yell and a high kick.

CHAPTER SEVENTEEN

There wasn't a lot of space to fight.

Scott backed up as the woman flew at him, tossing the tote bag onto the bed to have his hands free. She landed short but didn't break stride, spinning swiftly to deliver a high kick that also didn't connect. Stiletto ducked under the graceful swing of the woman's long leg, and slammed a balled fist into her abdomen.

The woman yelped and staggered to the side, avoiding the bed by shifting her direction. Stiletto shifted as well for another counterattack, but she leapt at him, colliding this time, slender fingers wrapping around his neck as they tumbled to the carpet.

Stiletto choked as her grip tightened, her wiry arms bulging with muscle, her eyes locked on him and her face twisted in a grimace. Her knees were locked against either side of his hips, but that left his arms free, although his reach was blocked by her arms. With an open palm, he managed to smack the side of her head, right against her left ear. Stunned, her grip loosened enough for Scott to run his arms between hers and force them apart, breaking the grip on his throat.

She punched him in the nose.

Now Stiletto saw stars. Then he saw her reach behind her back and bring her hand around with a short dagger. As the blade plunged at his chest, Stiletto raised his left arm to block. She pulled back for another thrust, and Stiletto shoved two fingers of his right hand directly into her throat.

The woman choked, eyes opening wide, her dagger thrust forgotten long enough for Scott to throw her off of him. She landed in a tangle of arms and legs against the bed.

Stiletto jumped up as she started to recover and slammed a foot into her stomach. She hit the floor again, Scott stomping on her left hand to pull the dagger from her grasp.

She retched into the carpet.

"Who are you?" Stiletto said. He wandered back to the discarded purse, picked it up, and shook out the contents on the carpet.

She grumbled something at him, the guttural sound from her throat.

Scott opened her wallet and looked at the New Jersey driver's license in the front window. He slipped it out for closer examination, holding it up to keep an eye on the woman as she remained on knees and elbows trying to catch her breath.

Stiletto let out a curse when he read her name.

"All right, Gabriella Noguera Suarez, if that's your real name, who's the big shot you came to see?"

This time she managed to form words, some of which Stiletto understood, questioning his parentage and manhood.

He laughed and collected her smart phone from the scattered purse contents.

"Take any good pictures lately?"

He swiped the screen and looked at the icons on the screen. Like many people, she had no pass code. It was not convenient to always type in a set of numbers or have the gizmo read your face when you needed to contact something *right now* in the heat of a crisis.

Stiletto pocketed the phone.

Beth in his ear. "Sierra Two?"

"Fine for now. I think I got an upper echelon cartel player here."

Mitch Lang said, "You're about to have a party, Sierra Two, we're almost there."

Gabriella Noguera Suarez started to rise, the red flush on her neck visible despite her olive skin, the anger in her eyes more than noticeable as Stiletto also pocketed her ID card.

Her eyes darted around the room.

"Forget it, Gabriella," Stiletto said.

But she didn't. Stiletto snapped the Colt .45 from leather as she lunged. He didn't want to fire. The unsilenced gunshot would bring more trouble than it was worth. He swung the barrel in a sharp arc, connecting with the side of Gabriella Noguera Suarez's head. The loud thud that resulted from the impact stopped her cold and she landed on the floor at his feet.

"Sierra Two?"

"Clearing the room, Bravo Charlie. Hostile unconscious."

The phone beside the bed buzzed.

Stiletto stowed his pistol and went to answer.

"Yes?"

"Sir, this is the front desk, we're getting a noise compliant from your room. Do you require any assistance?"

"My apologies. We dropped a suitcase."

"Please keep it down, sir."

Stiletto promised to do so and hung up. As he stepped over the woman's body, he nudged her with his foot.

"Hear that? You're disturbing the peace."

She offered no reply and only breathed shallowly into the carpet. Scott pulled her head up by her thick dark hair and used her phone to snap a picture of her face.

Stiletto grabbed his tote bag, transferring the cell phone and driver's license into the bag, and left the room. He casually strode down the hall.

"Bravo Charlie," he said.

"Copy."

"Making my exit. I keep getting into fights in hotels."

"Stay out of the elevators," Beth said.

Stiletto crashed through the stairwell door. "Way ahead of you." He started down the metal stairs, the echo of his steps bouncing off the walls.

"Any idea who she was?"

"Got ID and cell phone," Stiletto said, breathing hard as he descended the winding stairwell to the ground floor. "Middle name Noguera. She must be a family member. Sister. Daughter. Something. We'll get it sorted."

"Copy that," Beth said. "We got a good recording, by the way. See you at the rendezvous."

Stiletto acknowledged but let out a short laugh. Beth was trying to be fancy. Their "rendezvous" was nothing more than a typical "FBI surveillance van" parked in a garage two blocks away.

He exited the stairwell on the ground floor and hurried for the front doors.

He wanted to hear the recording of the meeting right away.

Stiletto ignored the parking attendant in the shack at the exit and found the white Ford Econoline van, side windows blacked out, parked among the rest of the cars in the garage. He communicated with Beth over the earpiece on his approach, tapping a code on the back door. Mitch Lang opened the rear door and Stiletto climbed into the cramped back.

The rig was set for full-time surveillance with a line of monitors on the driver's side wall, small chairs, and enough computer and sound equipment to film a movie, Stiletto thought. Beth sat in front of the gear, her pink purse / microphone / camera combo plugged into a USB port via cable, the images captured by the 4K camera on the line of monitors.

Stiletto sat on what amounted to a stool, and tried not to imagine the walls closing in on him. The van was a tight spot that could easily turn into a coffin. He said to Mitch Lang, "They get back to the hotel?"

Stiletto had only known Lang for a short time, but he'd already impressed Stiletto with his ability to blend into his surroundings. He was the Anonymous Man. Thin, bald, and wore clothes that looked like he'd picked them up from the floor in the morning and never bothered to iron.

"Yes," Lang said. "And if you left the woman there, they are probably a little upset right now."

"They'll be more upset when they find out what I took." Stiletto unzipped the tote bag and handed Beth the tablet, phone, notepad, and ID card.

She set the items aside and cued up the meeting at the mall food court.

"Here we go," Beth said. "Angle is a little wonky but we got all of them."

Stiletto examined the four men at the table. The shot was clear enough. Two Americans, one older, and two Latinos, all tough-looking characters, sat having their conversation over slices of pizza.

"Any ID?" he said.

"We have a name or two on the recording," Beth said, "and HQ is working on background."

Stiletto nodded. He noticed Greg Foster, the fourth member of their team, was missing.

"Where's Greg?" he said.

"He's following the Americans," Beth said. "Hopefully they travel straight to the go-between and we can wrap up this part of the mission."

"Never that easy," Stiletto said.

Beth said nothing and activated the playback with a sharp tap on the keyboard.

The ambient noise was limited, the voices of the four men loud and clear over the background chatter.

Stiletto, Beth, and Mitch watched and listened.

The Colombians shook hands with the two Americans, one introducing himself as Mr. Ross, the other as Mr. Kasson. The Noguera pair called themselves by first names, Eric and Henry, which were probably aliases. Headquarters would determine their real names, should their faces be on file anywhere. Stiletto figured they would be.

He leaned forward with his elbows on his knees and watched.

The conversation from the Colombian side went straight to business.

"We need a new connection in the United States, specifically to supply the East Coast with product."

Mr. Ross said, *"Mr. Kasson and I are very familiar with the product, so we know how to handle it."*

"Really?"

The older American spoke up. *"I worked with the agency in Los Angeles in the '80s. We handled the same product."*

The Colombians appeared impressed. *"But what about the publicity?"*

Kasson shrugged. *"Los Angeles was the only area of operations that was exposed. And shit happens. The difference here is that you'll have me in charge of a small group of people who will get the job done. You're not dealing with a giant bureaucracy that's trying to cover up the activity."*

"If we are going to do this," said one of the Colombians, *"we are going to need certain assurances. How you plan to receive and distribute, how we can transfer payment, that sort of thing."*

"I have something rough sketched out," the one called Kasson said.

"What is your idea?"

"How much product are you looking to move?"

The cartel man mentioned a number, and Kasson flinched.

"That's too much for a small operation," Kasson said. *"If we are going to avoid the problems you've already*

encountered with the Boston connection, we're going to need to scale down a bit. Keep the people involved to a minimum. We can still move enough to earn you the profits you're looking for, but they will be small profits that eventually add up to big profits, if you have the patience."

"We cannot afford a shortage in the market that might be filled by competitors," the cartel man said.

"We will have a dedicated squad to make sure that doesn't happen," Kasson said. "The market will be satisfied, I promise. I've done this sort of thing before."

"We will need to see a proposal. More details," the Colombian said.

"Fair enough. I suppose our mutual friend can forward it to you?"

"That will work. We will communicate through him. Have Mr. Rockwell contact us when you have your plan in final form."

"Won't be more than a few days," Kasson said.

"We look forward to it."

The meeting ended with handshakes and unfinished pizza left on the table.

"Got the lawyer name," Stiletto said.

"If it's not an alias," Mitch pointed out.

"Only one way to find out," Beth said. "We can ask Greg, and have HQ check him out."

Stiletto leaned back as Beth stopped the recording. He looked at his two teammates.

"Not a bad day's work," he said. "Can't wait to see

what's on the devices I brought in. May I have the cell phone?"

Beth passed it to him. Stiletto swiped the screen.

"No lock?" Mitch said.

"Nope. Let's see what pictures she's taken lately." He tapped the Gallery icon and the screen filled with pictures taken with the phone's camera.

Stiletto tapped on the first picture to enlarge the photo, and started swiping absently. Tourist shots. City shots. Selfies of Ms. Noguera Suarez. Lots of selfies of Ms. Noguera Suarez and Scott was about to make a remark about latent narcissism when he noticed a couple in the background that kept showing up in each of the selfies.

"Oh, no," Stiletto said. He swiped some more, his pulse quacking. He forced himself to slow and examine each picture. He found several others of the couple, and a lot more of only the wife.

The pictures showed the woman going about her day, running errands, working in the yard in front of a house.

Beth and Mitch leaned close to see what Scott was concerned about, and the color drained from their faces. The air in the van suddenly felt very stuffy, but Stiletto knew better than to ask Beth to crack a window.

The couple in the photos were General Ike Fleming and his wife. The pictures of the wife were more concerning, because there were no pictures of only General Ike.

Mrs. Fleming was under surveillance.

"Foxtrot to Bravo Charlie."

Beth Carrington snapped out of the shock of seeing Betsie Fleming in a drug cartel member's cell phone and answered Greg Foster's call.

"Here, Foxtrot."

"I'm at an office building—" he gave the address and Beth noted it down on a slip of paper. "It's mostly lawyers and architects. I don't know which office our two guys went into, but I have a directory of names we can check on."

Beth said, "Is the name Rockwell on the list?"

Foster paused a moment. He then said: "Yes. Rockwell, Travis & Beaumont. Fifteenth floor."

"Get back here as fast as you can."

"Copy."

The sat link fell silent.

Beth said, "We have to alert HQ and get these images transmitted to them for analysis."

"Of course," Stiletto said. He'd never seen Betsie Fleming up close, but there was no doubt it was the General's wife. The pictures of them together showed a couple that had been married longer than anybody expected from a man in the General's line of work.

The leak they needed to find must have been worse than the General, or Number One, realized, because how else had the enemy been able to get a fix on Fleming and his wife? Did he also have children that might be in danger?

Stiletto wasn't about to let anything happen to the man who had saved his neck more than once, and supported him even when it was the unpopular opinion around CIA headquarters.

And if the Noguera Cartel thought Fleming would be an easy target, Scott Stiletto was about to prove them fatally wrong.

Beth went to work with her gadgets while Stiletto called Fleming to update him and share the discovery. The General took the news of the surveillance photos stoically, but wanted to see them before he made any other comment. His thoughts echoed Stiletto's. The mole was buried deep, probably on the Colombia side of the operation, but finding the leak and permanently plugging it was second on the priority list. The first was stopping the Noguera Cartel from continuing its stranglehold on the East Coast of the United States.

"If you want to take me off of this and watch over you and your wife, sir," Stiletto said, "I'm happy to do that."

"I'm not making any decisions right now, short of alerting Betsie and arranging a watch. I will keep your offer in mind."

Stiletto said okay.

"How long till Foster returns?"

"Maybe a half hour."

"Get back here as soon as you can."

Stiletto thought he heard a hint of desperation in the General's voice, but dismissed it as a trick of his imagination.

CHAPTER EIGHTEEN

The quiet lobby greeted Edward Kasson and Perry Ross as they stepped off the elevator. A receptionist smiled as the two men approached. Her desk was placed against the left wall, around which were a pair of double doors. She was the lion guarding a cave entrance.

"Good afternoon, gentleman, do you have an appointment?"

Ross did the talking.

"Perry Ross for Adam Rockwell."

She didn't reach for the phone. "And your associate?"

"Edward Kasson. He's expected as well."

Now she picked up the phone, adding, "One moment," as she pressed two buttons. After a short wait she spoke into the phone. "Mr. Ross and Mr. Kasson are here for their appointment."

She hung up and gestured to a small couch against the opposite wall. "You may wait over there. Mr. Rockwell's assistant will be out in a minute."

Kasson sat and crossed his legs while Ross remained standing. They didn't hold those positions for very long.

The double doors next to the reception desk opened and another woman, a brunette who also wore a dark suit, asked the two men to follow her.

Beyond the doors the office bustled with activity, mostly confined to cubicles. The brunette stopped at the end of the hall, knocked on a door, pushed it open, and announced Mr. Ross and Mr. Kasson. She stepped aside for them to enter. Before Kasson knew it, she had shut the door, leaving them in a large office with a man rising from a large desk.

The man was positioned away from the windows overlooking the city. The windows acted as a wall between the inside and out.

"I'm Adam Rockwell." The man came around the desk, shaking hands with Ross and Kasson, saying to Ross, "It's nice to finally put a face to the voice on the telephone."

Ross agreed.

Rockwell was almost as tall as Kasson and well-built, his white shirt snug over broad shoulders and chest. He was no slouch in the exercise department, but Kasson doubted he could handle himself in a fight. Kasson also noticed he wasn't wearing a wedding ring, so the physique was part of his lady-catching formula.

Rockwell led the two men over to a sitting area and provided them with drinks, straight scotch of the 12-year-old variety, before sitting down.

"I trust the meeting went well?" the lawyer said.

Kasson didn't say anything. He let Ross do the talking.

"We've agreed to formulate a plan, and give you the information to forward back to Colombia."

"I can do that."

Ross said, "Who else are they talking to?"

"Just you, for now."

"What does that mean?"

"It means they're going to look at your proposal," Rockwell said, "and decide if it works for them. If not, they will move on to their next option. Which, admittedly, doesn't mean much. They've gone the route of the mob syndicate only to have that fall out from under them. They'd really like somebody on the outside, men such as yourselves, to facilitate their needs."

Kasson finally contributed to the conversation. "Part of what we have in mind is moving small amounts of the product instead of the big shipments they're used to. If we're going to do this properly, with as few people as possible, a big operation is out of the question."

"Are they aware of that?"

"We made it clear," Ross said. "They seem agreeable."

"Okay. Why don't you two get to work on the details, and have it ready for me Thursday. Will three days be enough?"

"We'll get it done," Kasson said.

"Great! Well, if there's nothing else…"

The trio finished their scotches and Rockwell escorted to the lobby. A round of handshakes and the two mercenaries were back in the elevator.

As they descended, Ross said, "What do you think?"

"I think they may not take the deal."

"You said you could make it happen."

"I can make it happen. It depends on whether or not they can scale down a bit, and I'm not sure they will want to. Cartel people aren't known for their subtlety."

CHAPTER NINETEEN

"Sorry I'm late."

Nobody around the table blamed General Ike for being slightly behind the eight ball. After what they'd discovered in New York City, he deserved a little slack.

Stiletto watched his boss. The General moved in a rush to the head of the conference table, setting down a tablet computer and two thick file folders before taking his seat. Behind him, hanging on the wall, was a large screen monitor, ready to display whatever the General wanted to show.

Already seated were Stiletto and Beth Carrington on one side, and Greg Foster next to Mitch Lang on the other. The conference room in the underground master control center of headquarters was adjacent to the operations room, and a glass wall offered a view of the activity, but none of the sounds from outside filtered into the meeting area.

Stiletto examined the General's face. He looked like

he hadn't had much sleep since the discovery of the surveillance pictures. The General folded his hands in front of him and addressed the agents.

"New York gave us a bit more than we bargained for."

"That's putting it mildly," Stiletto said. The other agents agreed. "What have you done to protect Mrs. Fleming?"

"Number One has offered a rotating team of security officers to stay at the house," the General said, "for now. We may relocate, or I may even bring her here. We're still talking about that."

Beth said, "We'll help with whatever you need."

"Much appreciated. For now, I think the best thing we can do is complete this operation and eliminate the threat entirely." He picked up the tablet and started tapping the screen. On the large-screen behind him, two faces appeared side by side. An older man with white hair on the left, and a young man on the right.

Stiletto frowned. The lower edge of the picture displayed a line of numbers, a code found on every ID card issued for those who worked at CIA headquarters.

"These are the two Americans who met with the cartel representatives," the General said, setting the tablet aside to consult the paper folders. He opened each one. "Perry Ross and Edward Kasson are former CIA officers. Both worked sensitive projects, and both have experience with the drug trade."

"I don't like the sound of that," Stiletto said.

"Kasson was part of the operation to flood Los Angeles with drugs and funnel the money to our Central American efforts in the '80s," the General said. He shook his head. It was one of the biggest black eyes in agency history, one that still haunted the agency and still talked about by those who wished to attack and undermine the CIA's efforts. "Ross is too young to have participated in that, but he also worked in Central America throughout his career, so his contact list must be huge."

"If they're former agents," Stiletto said, "what are they doing now?"

"Kasson is a mercenary," Fleming said, "apparently in high demand. Works mostly in Africa and Eastern Europe. Perry Ross is an organizer. Governments, corporations or individuals requiring mercenary work contact him, and he in turn contacts men like Kasson."

"I remember Ross's name from my Blackwater days," Greg Foster said. If Mitch Lang was the "anonymous man" then Greg Foster was the opposite. His shirt and jeans were pressed. He had a lot of hair on his head, sharply combed, and a goatee without a hint of gray despite being in his mid-40s. He could have spared some of the hair and donated it to Mitch.

"Ever cross paths?"

"No, sir. But my old boss might still know how to contact him if we need to."

"I will keep that in mind."

"Yes, sir."

General Ike tapped the tablet, and another picture appeared on the screen. The photo showed a well-built man with a smile on his face, leaning against the wall of a building, the sign beside him displaying the name of his law firm.

"Adam Rockwell, Esquire," the General said. "Spent most of his career as a criminal defense attorney before opening the firm he's at now with two other partners, and he hasn't seen the inside of a courtroom for at least ten years.

"Never married, sort of a local playboy," the General continued. "No known cartel associates, but plenty of domestic drug cases that might have put him in touch with the top layers of various cartels."

Stiletto said, "And the woman in the hotel room?"

Another tap of the tablet, another picture on the screen. The new photo showed a woman with long dark hair, wearing a tight party dress which accentuated every curve. She held a pink AK-47 at the hip, firing at stationary targets on a hillside.

"Gabriella Noguera Suarez," the General said, "is the sister of Amadis Noguera, current head of the operation."

"Sweet," Stiletto said. "Why was she here?"

Mitch Lang spoke up. "Visiting Rockwell, probably. Getting the scoop on the potential new hires."

"Could be," the General agreed. "What we're more concerned about is what was on the cell phone and other items Scott recovered."

"You mean the pictures of your wife," Stiletto said.

"And me."

"Of course, sir."

"There were some on the phone, and more on the tablets. The other phones have given us names and numbers to check out but we're not putting any stock in that information yet."

"And the hand-written notes?"

"Nothing exciting," the General said. "Just ideas for places to eat."

Stiletto suppressed a laugh, but once again felt surprise that bad guys needed to eat and sleep like everybody else.

The General stopped talking. He let out a sigh. Stiletto knew the discovery of the pictures was weighing on him. He wanted to help. There had to be a way to push General Ike into action, and get his wife out of the line of fire.

"We have names and faces," Stiletto said, "but now what?"

"Now what indeed," General Ike said.

The General glanced at each agent, and Stiletto felt awful. General Ike was a man used to living in the shadows, running the show from behind the scenes, out of danger, a chess master moving pieces across a board.

Now, he was caught in the crossfire of a compromised mission.

And Stiletto wasn't sure how to help other than to strike hard, strike fast, and eliminate the threat before tragedy struck. Stiletto had spent his career fighting for those who had no champion. His boss needed such a champion now more than ever.

He did too. The Trust had given him a gift, a chance to start over. He'd lost his family, but the Trust provided a new one. Stiletto wasn't going to let anybody take that away.

CHAPTER TWENTY

Stiletto said, "Here's how I see it."

All eyes, including Fleming's, turned his way.

If Fleming wasn't going to say what needed to be said, Stiletto would say it for him. "We have a security leak that has allowed the opposition to get close to our command personnel," Stiletto said. "General, if they can get close to you and your wife, they probably know about this base."

Nobody replied, but faces looked grim.

Stiletto continued. "Our first point of concern is protecting Mrs. Fleming and this headquarters. Can we beef up the security team?"

"Certainly," Fleming said.

"Secondly, the lawyer, Kasson and Ross, and the cartel. The usual drill. Gather information, and make our moves fast, because the enemy is already ahead of us. Prioritize targets and execute accordingly."

"I hope I don't sound like I'm speaking out of turn, but I agree with Scott's assessment," General Ike said. "I need to make sure my wife is protected."

Nobody disagreed. With Betsie safe, they knew the General could better focus on the second priority.

"We will bring her here even if Number One hasn't decided yet. At least, for now. Once we determine what shape we're really in, we can move her elsewhere."

The agents agreed.

"Anything else?"

Beth Carrington raised her hand.

"Yes, Beth."

"The elephant in the room, General," she said. "How did they know how to find you and your wife?"

"There is a traitor somewhere in the organization. Probably the same traitor that fouled up the mission when it was overseen by CIA."

"Somebody in the field in Colombia?"

"That's my assumption. It can't be anybody here at the Trust because the problem began long before Number One became involved."

"We might as well add a personnel review to our list," Beth said.

General Ike nodded. "I will manage that. Last call for questions?"

There were no more. Fleming dismissed the meeting and told them to remain on stand-by while he coordinated a pick-up with his wife. Stiletto noted, as he left, that the General remained seated.

Scott paused in the doorway, but the General spoke up

before he could say anything.

"I'm okay, Scott. Carry on."

Stiletto didn't believe the boss, but he also wasn't going to argue. He nodded and left Fleming sitting at the table.

Isaac Fleming was certainly *not* okay.

He and his family had never faced a direct threat before. Under the protection of the CIA, he'd been insulated, his name hidden from the press and classified. None of the mole hunts that had taken place during his career had involved the exposure of employee names or the names of upper management. Those moles had only been interested in peddling secrets for money.

But now, they had a mole that was more than willing to expose the Trust's command structure, and the entire east coast headquarters operation, to enemy guns.

He stared at the table top with his mind racing. He'd taken for granted that the same anonymity he'd enjoyed at CIA would cover him with the Trust. Obviously, that wasn't the case. He wasn't dumb enough to blame Number One. Even he was under threat, whether featured in surveillance photos or not.

They were dealing with an extreme situation, a rogue wave that had capsized the ship. The only thing to do was climb into the lifeboats and keep fighting for survival.

And as he sat there, General Ike thought about Beth

Carrington's remarks about the invisible traitor.

He hadn't been with the Trust long enough for many agents to know his identity.

Which meant that whoever pointed the Noguera Cartel at him and Betsie probably knew him already.

Which narrowed the suspect list. Somebody who knew him from his days at CIA. There couldn't be very many.

Fleming gathered his briefing material, turned off the large screen monitor, and left the conference room. His mind was still spinning, but with something that replaced fear. Instead, he was full of determination to narrow down the list of traitors and plug the leak once and for all.

CHAPTER TWENTY-ONE

"Are you sure it's best to bring her there, Isaac?" Number One said.

"Right now, sir," the General replied into his telephone while seated behind his desk. "I'm only sure of what day it is."

"It would have to be temporary."

"In case the base is under surveillance, absolutely. I need a little time to find another secure location, and until then I want her close by."

"Go get her then."

"Thank you, sir."

"I'm calling for reinforcements to the security team. They'll arrive tomorrow by bus."

"I've already spoken with the command sergeant and the crew is widening their patrol, looking for anybody watching us, all that."

"Keep your chin up, Isaac. We will overcome this and make them wish they'd never started this fight."

"From your mouth to God's ears, sir," Fleming said.

Stiletto hoped their little caravan didn't look too obvious on the highway.

He drove in the first vehicle with General Ike in the passenger seat, with Beth Carrington behind them in the middle seat. In the second SUV following them, Foster and Lang kept pace. The boosted Chevrolet Tahoes were faster than standard production thanks to bolt-on super-chargers and a custom engine tune, armored, with chassis-mounted countermeasures such as smoke and steel spikes, and racks for automatic weapons inside each door.

All Scott had to do was kick away a panel to have access to a fully-loaded Heckler & Kock MP-7 machine pistol, should the need arise. He hoped it didn't. The last thing he wanted was trouble while exfiltrating Betsie Fleming from her and the General's home in Woodstock to headquarters.

The Flemings had not lived in Woodstock very long. They had put their former home, in Alexandria, on the market as soon as the General took the job with the Trust. He had no intention of making a 2-and-a-half hour commute each direction every day. Woodstock was the compromise move, a town small enough for the quiet they wanted, but close enough to HQ and Alexandria where they could keep up with their social circle and Fleming had an easier drive to HQ.

They had an hour on the road each way, and plenty of firepower, but Stiletto hoped they didn't need to fire a single round.

The drive was comfortable enough, with two lanes in either direction separated by an island of land down the middle, traffic moderate and not too heavy. They traveled with a smattering of cars and heavy-duty trucks and semis.

Scott had not taken much notice of the route during his first drive along the highway with Beth Carrington, as it had been too dark. Now he took in the scenery. Mostly open space, country-land, farms here and there, collections of homes and businesses. A lot of green, which contrasted beautifully with the clear blue sky above.

Plenty of open space for one wanting to escape the noise of a city.

And plenty of spots for an ambush.

Stiletto took comfort in always seeing Foster behind the wheel of the other Chevrolet in the rearview mirror. Foster and Lang had proved themselves to him in New York, where their focus and professionalism spoke more to their abilities than a gun battle. They were good men to have on one's team.

Beth, of course, didn't need to justify herself to Scott. He'd seen her in action in some tough spots during the Venezuela mission. She'd earned his trust and respect forever.

Should they need to talk to one another, each agent had an earpiece com unit, same as in New York. The fit was so comfortable in Stiletto's ear, he almost forgot it was there.

The General sat in the passenger seat very stoically, still dressed in his suit and tie, while the operatives with him wore street clothes and street shoes and were ready to fight. The General's spit-shined Rockports wouldn't be a hindrance in a fight, but it was not ideal either.

Scott had not been privy to the phone conversation between him and his wife, but the look on the General's face suggested it had been quite frantic as his mind raced on how to gain his wife's support for the forced move with no estimated time of returning to normal.

"How much does she know?" Stiletto said.

"Sorry?"

"What does she know? About the Trust?"

"She's aware of my job. Like last time. She did not take the news well of what we're doing today."

"She knows there's a target on her back? I got the feeling from the pics she was more the focus than you."

"I had the same reaction," Fleming said. "But how do you tell your wife that?"

"I wouldn't know."

"I didn't mean—"

"Of course you didn't, sir. But that's still my answer."

General Ike let out a sigh. "Beth, any suggestions?"

"Not right now."

Stiletto glanced at her in the rearview. She wasn't watching them, may not have been listening. Her eyes were scanning side to side, watching for the same threats as Scott.

Stiletto slowed as he neared the tailgate of a big rig. Going slow, and being stuck behind civilians, was not the way he wanted to have to engage the enemy.

And that was Stiletto's biggest concern. Cartel operatives would not hesitate to open fire on an American highway, and have no qualms about killing civilians in their attempt to get to the Flemings.

Such a scenario had to be avoided. There was still a long drive ahead, and Stiletto's pulse rate remained elevated as his combat senses stretched out around him looking for signs of assurance, or threats.

CHAPTER TWENTY-TWO

The Flemings had a nice one-story home on Main Street in Woodstock, across the street from a Catholic church. The General said he liked the location because cops always said fewer crimes are committed around homes near churches because crooks are a superstitious bunch, which didn't make sense to Scott, but that was par for the course. Bad guys lived in their own world.

Stiletto parked in front of the house. The lawn was dry in spots, and Fleming said it was driving him nuts trying to revive the grass as he and Stiletto exited the vehicle. Beth moved to the driver's seat. Greg and Mitch parked across the street. Stiletto could see by the positioning of Foster's arms as he sat in the passenger seat that he'd released one of the HK MP-7s from it mount and held the weapon at the ready.

Fleming started up the stone walkway to the front door with Scott hanging back, scanning. Cars drove by. A dog barked somewhere. The fresh air was nice. No threats. All quiet. Stiletto followed his boss up to the porch.

There was no fence around the Flemings' home or around the surrounding homes. That wouldn't have sat well with Stiletto. He needed fences. And walls. He needed protection. Something between himself and the unseen enemies. Down the street, Stiletto noted some houses had several trees surrounding the structures, and that would do if nothing else was available.

He admired the General's ability to eschew such protections. Stiletto figured he'd be an even bigger proponent, perhaps one who might want an isolated home in the country with a moat filled with alligators and machine gun ports in the attic.

Fleming used his keys to unlock the front door and announced himself as he entered. Stiletto wished they could have brought the captured tablet computer and smart phones to show Betsie Fleming the true extent of the threat, but the devices could not leave HQ. Typical security measures, sure, but the pictures might have gone a long way to calm any initial reaction from Betsie Fleming.

It turned out no evidence was required.

She called to her husband from the back bedroom and Stiletto let the boss go to her while he checked the living room, looking out onto the back yard, which appeared to have no boundary and joined seamlessly with the house behind them and to the one on the side. Since the Flemings occupied the corner lot, the left side of the house as you entered the front door looked out on the street. Stiletto again saw nothing out of the ordinary, no cartel crew wagons waiting to pounce.

He continued through the house, checking each room, as the Flemings talked in the master bedroom. Mrs. Fleming was asking how much stuff she should bring for them both. She wasn't arguing at all. She took the situation seriously, and that made Stiletto grin. She was probably made of the same hard-charging stuff as her husband.

He stepped into the bedroom last, where his boss introduced him to his wife, then excused himself to check in with the others.

"All clear in the house."

"Clear outside," Beth said. "Any trouble with the wife?"

"She's only wondering if she's packing too much."

Beth chuckled. "She's been a spy's wife for a long time, I guess."

"Good way to put it."

After another few minutes, the Flemings emerged, each carrying two suitcases. They moved fast behind Stiletto as he held the front door open, and he remained there while Beth jumped out of the SUV to help them load. The General returned to lock the door, and by the time he and Scott climbed into the Tahoe, the engine was already running.

One more hour on the road.

Then, hopefully, safety.

CHAPTER TWENTY-THREE

Beth drove while Stiletto rode shotgun and the General and his wife sat in the middle row.

Betsie Fleming was certainly no dummy. After her husband explained where they were going and described the living quarters, she said, "If this drug army knows where your base is, are you sure it's safe for me?"

Stiletto cocked an ear. He had to see how the General talked his way out of that box.

"My boss doesn't even want you there, hon," he said.

"Then why in the world—"

"It's temporary. We're talking one or two days while I find another place not even my boss knows about."

"But if they're watching—"

"We've doubled our patrols, honey. We have more armed troops on base than I've ever seen, and they're scouring the area. They've turned up nothing, so we think we're safe as far as somebody camped out watching the base is concerned."

"Do they have a satellite?"

Stiletto couldn't stop the chuckle that escaped his mouth.

The General said, "Something funny, Scott?"

"If the cartel has access to satellite surveillance, we're in bigger trouble than we realize."

To his wife the General said, "No, they can't be watching us via satellite."

"What about a drone?"

The smile vanished from Scott's face. *This lady knows the drill. Too many movies or too many chats with the General?*

Fleming didn't respond right away. Beth glanced at Scott. Her face looked grim.

Because nobody had considered the possibility of a drone flight over the base.

The better drones could be launched from outside the headquarters boundary, and flown over the area to capture still and video images. And the drones didn't have to fly terribly high in order not to be noticed by those on the ground who weren't considering the possibility that they were up there to begin with, and they were small enough not to show up on radar. Headquarters security was concerned with big threats: airplanes and helicopters. *Had they considered small threats?*

"Opinion, Scott?" the General said.

"If they're using a drone, it's flying by remote, or a pre-programmed flight path," Stiletto said. "They'd only need to fly over once or twice a day to have enough footage to figure out what we're doing. If they happen to fly over and notice your wife, they'll know they have you both in one convenient spot."

Betsie Fleming said, "Maybe you should drop me at a motel."

"If they see us arrive," Beth said, "they might see us leave."

"Not if we institute immediate countermeasures," the General said.

"Like what?" Stiletto asked.

"We have missile launchers on-site," Fleming said. "Latest hand-held variety, though I'd prefer a battery of anti-aircraft rockets. I'll have the boys look for a drone and blow it out of the sky if they see one."

General Ike pulled out his phone and called the command sergeant at HQ. The conversation was short.

Thirty minutes to go. It had been a long day, starting with the mission in New York City, and now transporting Betsie Fleming to HQ. The sky was getting dark. The interior lights in the Tahoe had a muted glow.

Stiletto was too charged up to be tired, but knew he'd crash once they were back at HQ. He checked with Foster and Lang, who drove a few car lengths behind their Tahoe.

"Foxtrot, Lima, you two okay back there?"

"It was an easy ride, Sierra Two," Foster replied, "until somebody started talking about drones."

"Copy that," Stiletto said. If anybody else in the car detected a hint of exasperation in his voice, nobody pointed it out.

Nobody was perfect. Even professionals, trained warriors like Stiletto, Beth, Foster and Lang, could miss a detail with a slip up. The inevitable visit of Mr. Murphy always followed. What can go wrong, will go wrong. There might not be any drones flying over base. Mrs. Fleming probably watched too many movies or read too many Mack Bolan and Gray Man novels. The idea was something Stiletto and the others should have thought of, but they'd been too concerned, with resulting tunnel vision, of getting Betsie Fleming out of harm's way. They hadn't stopped long enough to consider how else the enemy might be watching them.

But at least they knew the enemy was only watching the Flemings. None of them, or any other Trust operative, had turned up in the surveillance pictures.

Scott almost wished *he* had somebody watching him, if only for a chance to strike back at whoever thought they were being so clever.

He had a family to protect. One not his own, but one he felt equally close to, and responsible for. He wasn't about to lose a single member.

Beth kept her foot solidly on the accelerator, goosing the throttle every time a semi or another vehicle pulled alongside. She also changed lanes, rather aggressively, if they came up on a slower-moving vehicle. She didn't want anybody riding too close to them. She didn't want to get stuck behind a slow poke. They had to keep moving, keep the area around them clear, to avoid potential danger spots.

Stiletto glanced at the clock on the dash. Time seemed to slow down. Twenty-five minutes till home. It felt like more than that had passed, and with the lack of light, it was getting tougher to watch the area off the road.

All he, all they, could do, was keep their eyes open and cross their fingers and toes.

New York City

"I'm not pleased, Adam."

Rockwell sank in his chair. Amadis Noguera hadn't made a threat of any kind, but the tone of his voice suggested otherwise.

"At least your people weren't killed," the lawyer said. He sat in his office with the lights low.

"I'm very happy for that, yes, especially my sister," Noguera said. "But it means our plans are in jeopardy."

"I don't think so," Rockwell said.

"Explain yourself."

"It might have been the Flynn people."

"Why?"

"They're upset you pulled out of the deal."

"Their organization is in shambles with the death of Giles Flynn. They should understand why I cancelled."

"They might understand, but they don't want that."

"They don't have a choice."

"I'm only saying perhaps they're the ones who interfered."

"Are you forgetting who killed Flynn in the first place?"

"One of his people, obviously," Rockwell said.

"Nothing obvious about it, Adam, you know better."

Rockwell swallowed. Did he? Or was Noguera thinking too hard about an incident that was relatively simple to explain?

"Not even the FBI knows who did it," Rockwell said. "They're focusing on Flynn's people."

"Because it's the path of least resistance," Noguera said. "That level of destruction wasn't planned by a street soldier looking to take over. No, Adam, we're dealing with something much bigger."

"You aren't thinking for one minute," Rockwell said, "that it was the CIA, are you?"

"They're here in Colombia trying to destroy me. Why not?"

"Well—"

"And if it wasn't the CIA, it was another organization called the Trust. Have you heard of the Trust, Adam?"

Rockwell suppressed annoyance. Noguera asked the

question like a parent talking to a two-year-old. If it wasn't for his money, the significant amounts of money being moved from cartel accounts to Rockwell's own pocket, the lawyer might have told Noguera to piss up a stick.

"No," the lawyer said.

"Then allow me to explain."

CHAPTER TWENTY-FOUR

"Are you listening?"

Rockwell said yes.

"The Trust is a private intelligence network that operates worldwide. After we upset the CIA effort in Colombia, the Trust took over."

"Why?"

"Because the operation director was ousted from CIA, then picked up by the Trust. They're continuing the plan while CIA recovers from its losses."

"Do we know who this man is?"

"Our sources have helped us keep an eye on him, yes," Noguera said. "And we know where their US headquarters is located."

"What does this mean to me?"

"It means, Adam, that it is not the Flynn people, it is not the CIA, we are being harassed by a private network with its own agenda. That's what's going on. That's why I'm upset. That's what you need to understand."

"You're saying—"

"They follow only their own rules, counselor."

"I suppose I should be careful."

"More than careful. Once they put a target on your back, they don't give up."

Rockwell needed to get Noguera back on topic, the topic of the new replacements for Giles Flynn.

"What about the two men I introduced your representatives to?" Rockwell said. "Have you had a chance to consider them?"

"They will do fine," Noguera said. "I especially like Kasson and his background. The other I can take or leave."

"A lot of the infrastructure will come from the other man, Ross."

"He's fine. They're both fine."

"You don't seem enthused."

"They're not potential sons-in-law, Adam. They are associates. I will want to meet them before we put our agreement in final form."

"I'll tell them."

"I'll be in touch."

The line clicked in Rockwell's ear. With a sigh of relief, Rockwell put the handset back in the cradle. He needed to vacate the office so the janitors could clean. He quickly packed his briefcase with the night's homework, most of which wouldn't get done, and grabbed his jacket. He wished he felt satisfied with the day's work.

Not today.

The next morning, Rockwell rose early, having slept surprisingly better than he'd expected. After dressing in another power suit with a black tie, he grabbed breakfast at a diner around the block from his office. He finished and lingered over a second cup of coffee while checking the previous night's baseball scores. When a hulk with white hair dropped into the booth across from him, he looked up with a cocked eyebrow.

"Are you following me, Mr. Kasson?"

The mercenary leaned forward. "You promised to get back to us this morning. I wanted to make sure you didn't forget."

"You haven't been forgotten." Rockwell put away his phone. "I spoke with our friend last night, and he is eager to meet both of you. Arrangements to be determined. I expect you'll be flying down by the end of the week."

"That works. Did you ask him—"

"You'll have to present your ideas to him personally. We didn't have time to cover that in our conversation."

Kasson frowned. "I'm getting a sense that something went wrong."

"Very wrong," Rockwell said, and explained the inter-ference by an outside party. He didn't go into the same ex-planation Noguera had provided. The mercenaries could learn about the Trust in their own time. To Rockwell, the group sounded like something out of a comic book. He wasn't quite convinced they were the real deal, though his review of what happened to Giles Flynn, which he had looked at the night before instead of doing his homework, had him leaning in the direction of taking the outfit seriously despite his attitude to the contrary.

"How much do these outsiders know?" Kasson said. "Did the guys we talk to get beat up, too, or just the woman?"

"Just the woman, so nobody braced the other two for information. They did, however, steal some portable devices. There's no way you'd be on any of them."

"What if they were watching the meeting?"

Rockwell shrugged. "I'm sure you can implement your own countermeasures, Mr. Kasson. You should be good at that sort of thing."

"I am," the mercenary said. "And thanks for the tip. Otherwise we might have found out the hard way."

Rockwell smiled. He pushed the half-full coffee mug away from him. "Want breakfast?"

"I'm good, thanks."

"I need to get to the office. Lots to do today."

The two men rose at the same time, Rockwell paying his bill at the cashier. He tried to ignore his shaking hands as he handed over his credit card, signed the receipt, and returned the card to his wallet. The situation with the cartel and the mercs was going to spin out of control. He knew it. He turned from the cashier to see Kasson surveying the crowd outside. Nobody appeared to be watching them, but Rockwell wouldn't know if they were. He wasn't trained in counter surveillance. Maybe Kasson would have better luck.

They walked out onto the street together and joined the hustling pedestrian traffic.

"You going to be all right?" Rockwell said.

"The only way to know if one was under surveillance," the merc said, "is to get out and see if a team reveals themselves. I know all the tricks. I might be getting too old to fight in the world's arm pit, but I still knew how to survive."

Kasson said good-bye and turned down an alley at a quick clip. Rockwell watched him go with people jostling him as they moved around him, the lawyer ignoring some choice words about his parentage from a few of the people. He started forward again. Straight ahead. Damn the torpedoes and all that. He'd spent many years avoiding trouble with the law, because he knew how to manipulate the law to suit his needs.

Noguera said the Trust played by their own rules. And Rockwell had no idea how to defend against that.

CHAPTER TWENTY-FIVE

Scott Stiletto entered the cafeteria and spotted Fleming and his wife at a corner table, sitting close, talking quietly. They didn't notice him enter, and he didn't disturb them. He grabbed a tray and a couple of plates and went through the breakfast line making his selections. Eggs, bacon, hash browns, wheat toast. A glass of apple juice and hot tea, his usual Earl Grey. He sat and ate out of view of the boss and his wife.

He wondered what they were talking about. He wondered if Betsie Fleming had had a rough night. He hoped not. He hoped the General found a better place to hide her until the crisis passed. He hoped they could *make* the crisis pass fast by eliminating the threat, because knowing you have a target on your back, when you're a civilian, can wreak havoc on one's mental state. He was sure Betsie Fleming was strong enough, but wasn't sure how long it might take that strength to crack under pressure.

Ultimately, Scott didn't want General Ike sharing his

pain. One dead wife was enough for them both.

People are easier to fight for than ideals.

He hadn't taken much time to reflect on the changes in his life since joining the Trust. It felt like a lifetime. Getting comfortable at the headquarters seemed to erase all of the baggage of the past few months since being forced out of the CIA, and he felt he was adjusting well. He liked it here, and the people. There was a lot he still had to learn, people to meet, but the change was a good one, and he knew he could thrive. He even liked his little apartment. It was cozy. A few decorations here and there, a little personalization, and he might not need to find a place in Woodstock (which had impressed him during his brief visit) or anywhere else. He wondered if living there full-time would be a problem when other agents needed to rotate on duty. He'd ask later.

A group of people, two women and a man, entered the cafeteria. He didn't know them. They were talking about their favorite television shows and he wondered if they worked in the nerve center below the building. He wondered if one of the women was Rose, the overwatch officer who'd guided him during his attack on the Flynn compound. He wanted to meet her and put a face to the voice. He wanted to know more about the people he was fighting with.

He dug into his breakfast and drank some juice. The chefs were very good. There was cheese mixed into the scrambled eggs. Not a lot. Just enough. The hash browns were seasoned to perfection and bacon never let you down.

"Eating alone is bad for your digestion."

Stiletto raised his head as Beth Carrington dropped into a chair across from him. Her plate contained a huge omelet.

"Where did you hear that?" he said.

"Read it on the internet somewhere." She started eating. Some of the omelet's filling spilled out. It was full of meat and chunks of potato.

"Have a good night?" he said.

"I spent a few hours getting Mrs. Fleming settled. She's taking it well. I'm surprised."

"She's supposed to be a nervous wreck?"

"She's not supposed to be so accepting."

"Why?"

"When you're married to a spy, life can be a little tough."

"You know from experience?"

"My father."

"I see."

"My mother would have horrible insomnia when he was out in the field."

"CIA?"

"Yeah. I thought with him there I'd be hired for sure, but I failed one of the entry exams. Number One hired me instead." She smiled. "*Much* better deal."

"How did you meet the old man?"

"He knew my father. I didn't ask how they knew each other. I went home to visit one weekend, and Dad and Number One were already in the middle of a conversation. He'd been waiting for me to arrive."

"We all find our place eventually," Stiletto said.

"Have you?"

"I have, yes."

"Was freelancing really that bad?" she said.

"It might have been better if the Russians weren't trying to kill me."

"I don't think so."

"Really?"

"I think you're somebody who needs to be surrounded by people. You're not an island. Nobody is."

"In the end I decided I needed help, yeah."

"Most people are afraid to ask for help."

"To their detriment," Stiletto said. "We need to know there's somebody we can talk to that's been through the same stuff as we have. It makes life a little easier."

She laughed. "I'm always stunned that warriors are so philosophical."

"There isn't a choice. We see the worst life can offer. There's a lot of crap we carry around." He added, "Some of us more than others."

She nodded and sipped some coffee.

They finished eating in silence. Scott noticed the General and his wife leave before he and Beth cleared their dishes.

CHAPTER TWENTY-SIX

The General leaned back in his chair and his face looked grim.

"What's wrong, sir?"

Fleming had called Stiletto into his office a few minutes earlier. Scott sat, waiting for the conversation to begin. He was either moving on to the next phase of the mission, or being detailed to help protect Betsie Fleming. Either set of orders was fine.

But Fleming remained silent. Eventually Scott had to speak to get the boss talking. He may have looked calm in the cafeteria during breakfast, happy that his wife was by his side, but his expression showed nothing but stress.

"Something with your wife?"

"She's okay," Fleming said, waving a dismissive hand. "Taking it better than I thought, though she thinks the shower in the quarters is too small."

"She's not wrong."

General Ike finally cracked a smile. "I suppose she

isn't. I suppose I should drop a few pounds so it's not so tight for me too."

Both men laughed.

General Ike took a deep breath. "Comments so far? Let's hear what you think."

"We've identified the go-between like you wanted," Stiletto said, "and we know the two mercs the cartel may make a deal with. I'd say the first part of our mission is accomplished. We need to keep tabs on Rockwell, tap his phone and all that, and see who else he talks to."

"In progress," Fleming said, "if not done by now, knowing our technical people. They truly are the best. What do you suggest we do next?"

"We need to find the leak and plug it. If they're going to target you and your wife, they can target any single one of us. We're all in danger, sir."

"I've advised our off-duty personnel of the issue."

"And I think the leak is somewhere in Colombia," Stiletto said.

"You read my mind."

General Ike finally shifted in his chair to rotate the desktop computer monitor in Stiletto's direction. Using his keyboard, he brought up three pictures, file photos of other operatives, he said.

"These three knew me while I was at CIA," Fleming said. "They're freelancers. They were working with us when the Agency was in charge of the Noguera mission, and once that went quiet, I brought them over to our side to continue the job. It made sense because they were already familiar with the plan and the environment down south."

"Only these three?" Stiletto said.

"It has to be somebody who knows my background. Unlike Number One, I'm not anonymous. They can tell Noguera that Ike Fleming is in charge of this new outfit called the Trust that's making all the trouble for you. After that, I'm not hard to find.

"Nobody else on the squad down there knew me at CIA. We weren't able to bring over everybody from the previous mission, so most of them are new people."

Stiletto examined the pictures. A female and two males. They weren't pretty pictures. No glamour shots for them. The faces reflected hard living and hard fighting. Faces lines with experience.

"There's Hollie Wilder on the left," the General said. "About fifteen years of experience. Former Marine, couple tours in the Middle East."

Hollie Wilder wore her blonde hair tied back in the picture. The only thing that stood out to Scott, other than her blue eyes, was a mole on her left cheek.

"The one in the middle is Tim Chapman, ex-special forces, airborne paratrooper, the whole bit. He worked with some private military contractors after his discharge before turning freelance and working for CIA on and off."

Chapman's blonde hair was shaggier than formal regulations might have allowed, but he wasn't in the army any longer. His eyes looked dull. He didn't see anybody; he saw through them. Stiletto flagged Chapman as his primary suspect for that reason. He didn't like the man's look. It wouldn't mean anything until he saw the man up close, but he'd seen the same look in other traitors, men so exhausted from playing both ends against the middle that it took a physical toll, and reflected on their countenance.

"The third," the General concluded, "is Ben Monaghan. He's the most recent member of the squad. When a few guys left after CIA pulled out, I needed him to fill some of the gaps."

Monaghan's hair was tinted red, as if he was a natural redhead but dyed his hair darker. His cheeks were also flushed red. He was a drinker.

"One man for multiple slots?"

"He's very good," the General said. "Irish paratrooper. Heavy weapons, explosives, communications expert. He can wear many hats, and most of them on very short notice."

"All right. We're going to Colombia?"

"Not *we*, you."

"What about Beth and the others?"

"They'll be tasked with helping my wife, and covering the lawyer. We aren't letting Rockwell out of our sight even for a minute, now that we've found him."

"What's my mission?"

"Plug the leak. I'm not worried about Noguera, right now. We know where he is."

"Are you sure you don't want me here, sir?"

"I understand where you're coming from, Scott." That fatherly tone again. One Stiletto didn't think he'd hear again. But he *was* hearing it again and that made him feel good. "You would certainly be an asset. I can send somebody else to Colombia, no problem. But I know you're the best man for the job down there. Plus, by being there, you're helping to solve the problem of keeping my wife safe, not merely treating the symptoms."

Stiletto nodded. There was no need for further discussion.

He had his mission, a set of targets, and the backing of an amazing organization. He had a home, and new friends, waiting for him on his return.

He wasn't going to let General Ike down.

CHAPTER TWENTY-SEVEN

Boston, Mass.

Giles Flynn wore his best suit to the funeral.

Mrs. Giles Flynn, Barbara, had made sure to pull the double-breasted black suit he'd liked from the closet. It hadn't been worn in a while and needed a cleaning but she said the hell with it, Giles was dead, and the worms would be eating through the fabric within a year anyway so who has time to clean anything? She didn't want to fuss with a shirt and tie, so she grabbed a gray turtleneck and told the undertaker to make it work. His response was a curt, "Yes, ma'am," because even the undertaker knew who she was and what power she now wielded.

Flynn lay in the open coffin, his arms folded across his belly, looking like a fat and bald Illya Kuryakin. Barbara might have laughed if her heart wasn't so heavy. Despite her sarcasm and irrelevance, she missed the old bastard. He hadn't deserved to end the way he did. Other guys, yeah, screw 'em, but Giles, no way.

Maggie and Tammie, Mrs. Flynn's twin daughters, stood on either side of her, sobbing quietly, reaching under their black veils to dab their eyes. She stood stoically and stared at her husband's corpse. The undertaker had done a great job filling all the holes in his body, almost making it look like Giles died of natural causes. She'd been especially concerned about the bullet wounds in his neck, but whatever putty filled those holes vanished under the make-up used to give Giles Flynn that "only sleeping" appearance.

She held her daughters close as they sobbed, but no tears stained her face. There was only one thing on her mind. Finding the son of a bitch who did this, and tearing out his intestines.

But first, she had a duty to perform.

She and her daughters had been allowed in the chapel first to say their good-byes, and now stood back while the line of attendees passed the casket to bid their own farewells and then passed her and the girls on their way to their seats. The Flynn women made appropriate remarks to the guests, Barbara only when the girls found themselves speechless. Any other day, Barbara would have told the palookas to park their keisters and stay quiet, but she figured she had to let them do their thing, even if some of them might be plotting against her for the big chair.

She escorted her weeping daughters to the front row of the chapel, which had filled front to back with well-wishers, friends, and probably two or three FBI agents who wanted to catalog everybody who showed up for a gangster's funeral.

It was one of those non-denominational chapels at a cemetery because the last thing Giles Flynn ever thought of was a higher power. He wouldn't want any religious symbolism. Barbara couldn't stop those wandering around with a rosary, that was their business, but it didn't stop her from giving them the stink eye if they came within range. They were the wives of the other top guns in the Outfit, so they gave the eye right back to her.

Whoever designed the chapel, though, only thought in shades of brown. The carpet was brown, the pews were brown, the walls were paneled in brown, with nooks for candles and faux-stained glass. Overhead fluorescent lights only added to the monstrosity.

She'd have liked it much better if Giles had wanted to be cremated. Then she and the girls could scatter his ashes wherever and be done. No need for this parade of waste paying respects.

Barbara Flynn sat between her daughters on the hard wood of the pew which made her rear end hurt. She didn't have a lot of padding, and her bony backside was paying the price.

The music stopped and the funeral director took his place at the podium. He was a skinny chap in a cheap suit with slicked back hair. He was suitable enough. Barbara wasn't expecting a professional MC to do the honors.

The memorial program was simple. He'd say a few words, she'd go up and say a few words, anybody else who wanted would say a few words and if they went on too long Barbara would give them *The Look*, and they'd dismiss to the adjoining cemetery where they'd put Giles' fat Irish ass in the ground and then get on the phone to Colombia because if the wetbacks thought they were going to get away with cutting her family out of the drug arrangement they had another thing coming.

The "war" for Giles' chair wouldn't last long. Already men loyal to her were putting down the rebellion by any means necessary. If somebody even dreamed of taking the chair that now belonged to Barbara, they were getting whacked. And plenty of bodies had already been stacked. The seat was Barbara's. After her, one of the daughters would get it, and that was the line of succession, end of story.

Tammie kept tugging at her short skirt as the funeral director droned on. She and Giles had nicknamed her The Curse and today was yet another example of why. Her skirt was too short, her heels too long, and her lips too red for proper mourning despite the tears. She couldn't handle one day not dressing like a ten-dollar hooker.

Bless her heart.

The other daughter, Maggie, aka The Blessing, the one who behaved herself and didn't give her mother a heart attack every time she left the house, looked quite modest in her outfit, which included sensible heels and a full-length dress similar to her mother's.

When she finished addressing the guests, only two of the men came up to say anything, and they'd grown up with Giles and claimed to know him better than anybody. Barbara let them have their fantasy.

She was the only one who truly knew Giles Flynn.

CHAPTER TWENTY-EIGHT

The limousine door shut with finality and blocked out the rest of the world.

Barbara Flynn sat between her two daughters, who were still sobbing. She smacked their knees. "Stop crying."

Seated across from her was one of her husband's lieutenants. Now he was *her* lieutenant. Hunter Doyle, a thin man, who did not remove his sunglasses.

The limo pulled away from the chapel and out onto the street. They'd put Giles in the ground without incident, albeit with a few more speaking about their favorite memories, and somebody singing a hymn. The singing was off-key. A waste of time. *Typical.*

She said to Doyle, "Are we any closer to discovering who killed my husband?"

The girls had indeed stopped sobbing, but Maggie, the Blessing, kept wiping her eyes. The other girl, Tammie, stared out the tinted window.

"We caught his face on the house surveillance cameras," Doyle said, "and ran it up the flag pole. He matches the description of a man wanted for questioning in Washington, DC, over a shooting there."

"What kind of shooting?"

"He might have shot a man in an elevator. The local cops had the case, then the FBI swooped in and took it away from them, and then buried it."

"Why?"

"Presumably because he's an American agent," Doyle said.

"What kind of agent?"

Doyle shrugged. "Black ops? Who knows?"

"Why are black ops people targeting our organization?"

"Your guess is as good as mine, ma'am."

"Probably the Colombians," Barbara said.

"All the more reason—"

"Right. All the more reason for me to call Noguera and find out why he thinks he can cut us off like we're a weed or something."

Doyle didn't get flustered under her sharp gaze. "We'll keep searching for the shooter," he said.

"You better find him," Barbara Flynn said. "I want that man's head on a platter for the sake of my children." She patted the girls' knees this time. Neither twin spoke.

Stiletto waited alone.

A gentle breeze moved the trees around him, the leaves rustling quietly, creating a serene environment in which he could think.

He wore street clothes. No need for combat gear yet. The packs on either side of him contained clothing appropriate for the conditions in Colombia and his weapons.

He had two goals in Colombia, the primary being the discovery of the mole who was making the operation, and the lives of General Ike and his wife, more difficult than anybody wanted. His second goal was to smash the Noguera cartel.

But destroying one cartel wouldn't end the drug problem in the United States. Too many cartels had been beaten, only to be replaced by others who picked up the slack. It was a never-ending war, nearly useless, but if they didn't fight, the US would be flooded with narcotics. They couldn't have that, either. The best they could do was keep the flood at bay, despite the feeling that the dam was always springing a leak.

In the open field ahead lay a helicopter landing pad. The chopper would arrive soon to whisk Stiletto to a private airfield where a jet waited to take him to Colombia, and whatever lay ahead.

Once more into the breach.

"Scott."

Stiletto turned and found General Ike approaching.

"The grass isn't good for those shoes, sir."

"A shoe shine is cheap," the General said. He stopped and put his hands behind his back. "I have news."

"Okay."

"We learned something from tapping Rockwell's phone. He called Kasson and Ross. They're going to Colombia. In fact, they might arrive before you."

"I'll add them to the list."

Stiletto waited for the General to say more, but Fleming's eyes lingered on the landscape instead.

"Something else, sir?"

"We never know, do we?"

"I don't follow."

"Traitors. We never know who they might be. Any one of us might go the wrong way."

"Not all of us, sir."

"I know I can count on you. But only you, and that's what bothers me. How much do I share with other people that might come back to haunt me?"

Whipping rotor blades in the distance. The chopper was almost there. Scott didn't have time to console the General the way he'd like, so he boiled his argument down to something simple.

"The only choice is to cut those people out of your life, sir, and that makes for a miserable existence."

The General turned to Scott. "I think you're right."

"If you want me to stay—"

"Beth and Greg and Mitch can handle the situation here."

"Yes, sir."

The chopper flew over the tree tops, circling the open field, and carefully settled on the landing pad. The rotor blades did not stop. The wind generated whipped the trees back and forth. The men held up an arm to block flying debris, and had to shout over the noise.

"I won't let you down."

"Be careful."

Stiletto grabbed his packs. "See you in a few days!"

It was an optimistic farewell, but Stiletto wouldn't allow a single defeatist thought into his mind. It's what separated the winners from the losers.

The General raised a hand in good-bye. Stiletto hustled across to the chopper. The co-pilot had the side door open and helped Stiletto load his bags. Then Scott climbed into the cabin, and the co-pilot shut the door before returning to his seat.

Stiletto watched Fleming get smaller as the chopper rose, then the nose dipped and they flew forward. Then Stiletto only saw trees. But the image of Fleming standing alone in the field, probably feeling more alone than Stiletto ever had, stayed in his mind.

CHAPTER TWENTY-NINE

Stiletto had twenty minutes until the chopper arrived at the airfield. He spent the time using a tablet computer to go over the files on the General's suspects.

Chapman still looked like a good suspect because of his eyes. They were the eyes of a man used to duplicity. Stiletto couldn't quite explain the feeling, but his gut told him he was right. That didn't mean he wouldn't check out the others, but Chapman was first on his list.

The file noted that Chapman was the team leader in Colombia, having moved over to the Trust team from CIA. There were ten operatives total, all engaging in a covert battle against the cartel, sabotaging growing fields, processing plants, sniping at cartel troops and commanders. A harassment campaign while the top dogs back in the US sorted out the situation regarding the go-between. With that solved, Stiletto was confident they could move from harassment to full-scale assault. He was counting on it.

The General had told Stiletto, prior to his departure, that Chapman was fully briefed on Stiletto's arrival, and knew about his mission.

It was bait to see if and how he spread the news.

The chopper began its decent to the airfield. A white Cessna Citation Mustang waited on the airfield. Stiletto was very familiar with the jet, and hoped they had beer aboard.

Somewhere in Colombia

Amadis Noguera gave the putter a spark of movement, tapping the Titleist across the smooth tiled floor and into the tipped over cup about three feet away.

He was in the open-walled lounge of his estate, surrounded by the sounds of a waterfall, streaming sunlight, and bright green foliage all around. He retrieved the golf ball and repositioned further away than his previous shot. Addressing the ball, he brought the putter back and forward, a little harder tap on the ball this time, and watched it travel the distance only to stop short of the cup.

A little harder. He picked up the ball again and returned to his spot. Always a little harder. A bit more effort. That was the story of Noguera's life. If he wanted something, he had to work for it, and often fell into the "two steps forward, one step back" way of doing things. He took it in stride. He always reached the goal, even if it took more time than he figured.

"Don't you have something important to do?"

Noguera looked over his shoulder at the doorway to the lounge, where his sister stood.

Gabriella Noguera Suarez still had a few bruises from her fight with the American, but she hid them well. The welts on her face, covered by makeup, were only visible if you knew they were already there. Otherwise her touch-ups were quite thorough. She folded her arms. Her long dark hair hung well below her shoulders and was perfectly straight.

Amadis returned to his pose. "This is important."

Tap.

A little harder this time, and the ball made it all the way to the cup, but stopped at the rim of the glass and bounced back.

Amadis straightened and let out a quiet curse.

"Put that away. We have a meeting to prepare for."

Amadis ignored his sister as she walked into the center of the lounge, where all the furniture was, and dropped onto a couch, crossing her long legs, her arms folded once again, her eyes narrowed in frustration. The open floor surrounding the furniture was usually used for a food spread when they were entertaining. Screens covered the open areas at night and when it rained but, thankfully, the weather was nice enough that those screens weren't required now.

Amadis Noguera parked his putter in a corner and

helped himself to a drink from a nearby wet bar. He carried the bourbon, straight, to the sitting area and grinned at his sister as he took a sip. He sat down across from her, sinking softly into the cushions of the plush leather couch. Despite having owned the couch for a couple of years, the leather still smelled fresh.

"Why are you so upset?" he said.

"We have problems."

"We do indeed. We will handle those problems. After my last chat with Rockwell I'm very much looking forward to seeing Kasson and Ross, and we can add our own input and see what they want to implement."

"Who attacked me?" she said.

"I've given you the best answer I can," Noguera said. "We know the organization the man came from, but specifically identifying him will be a little tougher."

"We know where they're hiding, right?"

"Yes."

"We need to strike back. Wipe out the team harassing us."

"And what about my source? He will be exposed."

"Kill him too," Gabriella said.

Noguera downed his drink and rose to get a refill. "What good is my word then?" he said. The liquid splashed into the glass. "If I sacrifice my valuable players, how do I replace them?"

"He won't be working with this Trust group forever."

"Long enough."

"Then kill the wife of the leader. We've been watching her for a reason, right?"

"Funny you should mention that." Noguera returned to the sitting area. "You kept too many pictures on your devices, Gabriella. That mission is blown. The wife has been hidden away."

"Where?"

"Don't know. We won't unless my source says something."

"What about the base?"

"I don't think the man in charge would take the risk of keeping her there." Noguera drank some more bourbon and let it roll around in his mouth. He swallowed. He watched his sister pout at the carpet. "And besides, all we have to go on is our source's description of the place. We don't have anybody there watching. Unlike the American government, we don't have our own satellites in the sky that can watch you sunbathe on the beach. Be patient, Gabriella."

She scoffed.

"You aren't papa's little girl anymore."

"Gee, I wonder why *that* is."

Noguera shrugged. Not everybody knew he murdered his own father to get the top spot in the cartel, but those who didn't have direct knowledge certainly suspected him. Including Gabriella. She was not only a haughty firecracker to contain, she might also try to kill him if she ever discovered the truth.

But he didn't think she would do the actual killing. She'd get somebody else to do the deed, though she might be in the room to watch.

That's why Noguera needed golf, and putting practice. It kept his mind off how many gunsights he had on his back.

Being a cocaine kingpin was *not* an easy life.

CHAPTER THIRTY

Noguera and his sister watched each other like two lions poised for battle and waiting for the other to make a move.

The silence was broken by a door opening.

"Excuse me," said the chief of the house guard, a man named Humberto. Under his loose-fitting white shirt, he wore a heavy-caliber revolver. His graying goatee marked him as older than Amadis.

Noguera turned in his seat. "Yes?"

"She is on the phone."

"Who?"

"Mrs. Flynn, from Boston. She wants to talk."

Noguera rose and approached Humberto with his hands behind his back. "Why?"

"She says she wants to talk about keeping the agreement you made with her husband now that she has taken over the organization."

Noguera laughed. Even Gabriella found that funny.

Noguera straightened. "Let's hear what she says." He

crossed the room to a table where a landline telephone sat. He picked up the receiver and said, "Amadis speaking."

The Flynn woman's shrill voice blared through the phone. "How dare you!"

"Mrs. Flynn, my deal was with your husband."

"I'm in charge now," Barbara Flynn said. "The deal can still be honored."

Noguera swallowed some bourbon and laughed. "You aren't capable of performing at the same capacity as your husband, dear lady."

"Don't think you can brush me off like that!"

"Our arrangement is done. I know how the mafia works. You are going to be too busy defending your turf to deal with my business. Be gone with you."

"You're underestimating me. Same as my husband did all these years."

"I am done talking with you."

"Do not hang up—"

But that's what Noguera did, setting the receiver down with a chuckle.

"Why bother talking to her if you're going to tell her that?" Gabriella said. She was still on the couch, watching everything like it was a Mexican soap opera.

Noguera returned to the bar and considered yet another refill, but set the glass on the bar in disgust. The last thing he needed was a hangover.

"I was doing just fine until a bunch of women started bothering me," Noguera said. "Please leave me alone." He found his putter and the Titleist and stood six feet away from the cup. Placing the ball on the floor, he assumed the position and concentrated on making the shot. He tapped the ball with what he considered the proper amount of force. The ball rolled across the floor and clinked into the cup. He smiled.

Noguera didn't know when Gabriella finally left, but when he looked up, she was gone.

But Gabriella wasn't far away. She marched down the hallway toward the other side of the estate where her rooms were, with Humberto beside her.

"How much longer are we going to wait?" the house guard said.

Gabriella's face might have been granite for her lack of expression. "Not yet."

"When?"

"We need to see what the Americans are going to do. If I outright kill my brother, the whole cartel will rise against me."

"The Americans aren't doing anything except playing Boy Scout in the jungle."

"Give it time. A little more time."

"He killed *your* father. And *my* friend."

"I *know* that. But the dish isn't cold enough, Humberto."

The dish had been cooling since the day her father's

body had been discovered. She immediately knew what happened, who was responsible, but discovering evidence of what she instinctively knew took longer. Much longer than she'd anticipated. Amadis had the undying loyalty of many men in the cartel who knew he was guilty.

But every man has his price. Eventually, Gabriella found one willing to talk. He told her everything. And then she shot him through the left eye.

When the American CIA, and then the organization known as The Trust, began its operation against her brother's cartel, Gabriella seized the moment. She still had a role to play, a cover of her own to keep, because she was next in line for leadership should Amadis fall, and she played her part well. But she also passed along information to the Americans. Unfortunately, she didn't know everything. She had no idea who the mole in the commando group was. Amadis kept that secret to himself. But leaving her devices exposed in her hotel room, where she'd hoped the Americans might search upon their visit to New York, had been no accident, her fight with the American in the room a performance that carried a certain amount of risk. The man certainly knew how to hit, and she still felt the impact of his blows.

She'd help where she could, until she was standing over her brother's dead body, vengeance finally hers, and took his place. Then she'd have to fight the Americans herself. Her "allegiance" to them also served the purpose of learning their strategies.

"I'm tired of waiting," Humberto said.

"So am I," Gabriella said.

But soon. I can feel it.

Back in Boston, under the watchful eye of Hunter Doyle, Barbara Flynn sat behind her husband's desk at the Flynn Club. She locked eyes with Doyle, who offered no comment on the one side of the phone call he had observed. And she asked for none.

Barbara Flynn silently vowed that her connection with the Noguera Cartel wasn't over by a long shot.

Trust Headquarters

Beth Carrington found herself counting the hours since Stiletto's departure. She was worried about him, and didn't mind admitting it. He was once again charging alone into dangerous territory and she wished she was there to back him up.

But orders were orders. Stiletto had his mission, and she had her mission, which, right now, meant keeping an eye on Betsie Fleming.

She stood outside the barracks building looking skyward, watching for drones. She probably wouldn't be able to see any, but the clear sky and bright sun meant it was perfect "drone weather" or whatever was necessary to fly once of those things. The gee whiz crew below ground hadn't found any evidence of automatic flyovers, but Beth wasn't convinced that meant there hadn't been any previously.

Trucks rumbled along the open ground as the security crew maintained their activity, rotating in teams to patrol the forest and look for hostile forces. They'd turned up nothing, as well. No cartel killers hiding behind fallen tree logs, no sign of surveillance. Beth was glad the force had been increased, though finding places for the extra crew to sleep was tough, and an area behind the barracks had been cleared for tents and an outdoor living space that the troops claimed was a heck of a lot better than the sand box on the other side of the world.

She was waiting for Mrs. Fleming to emerge so they could take a walk around the grounds and Beth could keep the woman away from the dangerous places. Beth smiled hearing Mrs. Fleming say the words again. She didn't mind a stroll. It would take her mind off other things.

When the General's wife came down the steps on the side of the building, Beth noted she was dressed in jeans and a thick blouse, and wearing boots. She'd packed well. The afternoon already had a chill to it.

"Let's go walk around the helicopter pad, can we?"

"It's far enough away from the security teams, sure," Beth said.

They started walking. Beth wondered what General Ike had in mind for relocating his wife to somewhere safer.

"He's still working on that," Betsie answered. "I think he'll have a better idea when we get back."

They passed the building and started across the field.

"How did you get into this business, Ms. Carrington?"

Beth's thoughts stumbled for a moment.

It wasn't exactly the kind of question she wanted to answer.

CHAPTER THIRTY-ONE

Beth told Betsie exactly what was on her mind. "That's not really a question I want to answer."

"Too sensitive?"

"No, just boring."

Betsie Fleming laughed. "Oh, honey, if you want to hear something *boring*, I'll tell you how Isaac and I met."

Beth said, "Well, I grew up in New Hampshire. A lot of my family was in government, working in DC and all that, so I was always surrounded by politicians and this and that government person and it was all very … interesting, when I was a teenager. I went into the army for a while, then tried to get into the CIA and they said no, and now I'm working for your husband in this little secret program we have."

"That's not government-operated."

"Not at all," Beth said. "I like it better that way."

They walked in silence out to the helicopter pad, which didn't seem to hold Betsie Fleming's interest. They walked a little further. Beth grabbed Betsie's arm midway between the forest and the helicopter pad. "We should turn around."

"Why?"

"I know our security teams have said there's no cartel people hiding in the forest, but I'm afraid there *are* cartel people hiding in the forest."

"We better turn around then."

They started back.

"So how did you meet the General?"

"I don't want to bore you, dear."

"Then tell me this," Beth said. "How in the world did he get the nickname 'General'?"

Betsie Fleming laughed. "There isn't enough time left in the world to tell you *that* story."

En route to Colombia

Perry Ross glanced across the cabin at where Edward Kasson sat in a reclining chair near a window. Traveling by private jet was nothing new to Ross, who did it frequently, but the older, white-haired mercenary had stated it was not something he often experienced, so the first thing he liked to do was climb into the most comfortable chair on board and doze off. Kasson had accomplished his goal.

Ross worked a nail file over his fingernails as he sat in a comfortable leather seat of his own. He'd pulled down the shades on the window behind him because he didn't like the sun's glare. The lights in the cabin were fine for what he needed. He wasn't going to get his usual manicure with all this Colombia business, so as he rubbed away, he thought about their destination and the upcoming meeting with Amadis Noguera.

According to the lawyer, Rockwell, the cartel leader was looking forward to their proposal for moving Noguera product into the United States, but still upset and unsure of how to progress with an unknown threat hanging over them, as in, who shot Giles Flynn?

Ross didn't have an opinion on that, and laughed at Rockwell's description of the mysterious "Trust" behind the Flynn killings. He knew of no such organization, and didn't think a bunch of old timers unable to hang up their guns would be much of a threat to anything or anybody. They should be more concerned with their blood pressure and cholesterol. Ross had worked in the intelligence community for a long time, and knew of nobody who, upon retirement, wanted to get back into the game. When they were out, they were out.

The deal with the cartel truly intrigued him, and he had to fight to keep dollar signs from spinning in front of his eye. He figured the arrangement might last a couple of years, keep him busy, and result in what guys like him called the "retirement score" where once the job was over, they didn't have to get another. All of that assumed, of course, the DEA didn't catch on, US special forces didn't whack him, and nothing else went wrong with competitors. Any or all of those scenarios was within the realm of possibility.

Ross looked up sharply when Kasson started to snore.

Ross still had plenty of connections to redirect any heat, Rockwell certainly knew people in the DEA more interested in kickbacks than drug enforcement, and if they didn't get greedy, they might beat the odds and live to be as old as Kasson and snoring in a chair.

But one cannot count on luck to see them through an adventure. The deal also wasn't closed yet. If they couldn't reach agreeable terms, there was nothing to worry about. If they did form the alliance with the Noguera people, there was still time to plan a proper countermeasure strategy should they require one.

Presently the plane began its descent into El Dorado International Airport in Bogota, and Ross called Kasson's name to wake him up. The older man didn't budge. When the plane finally touched down on the tarmac, the jolt shook Kasson awake, who then chided Ross for letting him sleep so long while rubbing the fog out of his eyes.

They cleared customs without incident. Neither had brought any weapons. They were attending a friendly meeting, not knocking over the government.

They were met outside baggage claim with a Noguera driver holding up a sign with their names written on it. Ross decided the cartel knew how to treat a potential associate well when they climbed into a limousine equipped with a full bar.

He could get used to this.

CHAPTER THIRTY-TWO

The flight attendant shook Stiletto's shoulder. He woke with a start.

"We're landing in twenty minutes," the woman said. She smiled and Stiletto sat up in his chair, buckling his lap strap, and taking a peek out the window on his right.

The Cessna's engines droned quietly, light turbulence shaking the plane, but the beauty of Colombia stretched out below, and Stiletto noted a mass of scattered clouds over the region. He tried to remember the last time he'd visited Colombia, and remembered that his arrival hadn't been as nice. The last time, he and twenty other Green Berets jumped out of a Hercules and parachuted into the jungle. It didn't matter where; in Colombia, one part of the jungle was the same as the other.

He checked his phone for the local weather. Sixty degrees and scattered clouds. *Fair enough.* Humidity 60%. *Yuck.* He put the phone away.

At the front of the cabin, near the cockpit door, the

flight attendant took her own seat and buckled her seat belts for the landing. Stiletto tried to remember her name, but it had slipped his mind. Jenny or Penny. Something like that. She was a trained operator acting as the armed escort for the flight. Prior to showing him to his seat, she'd revealed the hidden compartment near here that contained automatic weapons and body armor. Just in case.

Scott recalled many of those "just in case" moments when a plane had been shot out of the sky only to be met with hostile forces on the ground. Venezuela, with Beth Chapman beside him, had been the most recent example. He wondered what she was doing. He hoped she wasn't getting bored. He didn't think Beth was the kind of operator who'd take kindly to sitting around for very long, and keeping an eye on Betsie Fleming might indeed entail a lot of sitting around.

The Cessna pilots stopped the plane at a private hanger, where customs officials met Stiletto for the immigration check, which gave Scott a chance to start work on his cover story of a private investor visiting Bogota to research Colombia's petroleum reserves. Petroleum was Colombia's main export, and Stiletto knew a little about the oil business from a long-ago mission in Saudi Arabia, so the cover was solid enough. Anybody checking on Stiletto's references would find that he was a reputable member of the oil industry, having written several articles on Middle East speculation efforts as well as having dated the daughter of an OPEC official with a very pubic breakup.

Evidence of which was manufactured by the Trust's technical section, and their work continued to impress Scott.

As Stiletto cleared customs and continued through the main airport terminal, he thought that if Colombia's oil export ever grew to more than 45% of the nation's exported goods, the United States might finally find a reason to invade.

Scott wondered where the mercenaries, Ross and Kasson, were in terms of their arrival time. Had he beat them to the country? Would they unknowingly cross paths in the terminal?

The El Dorado Terminal was certainly busy enough, and impressively built. Scott had never seen it before. It was another glass-and-steel structure that looked big enough to fit all of Texas and a portion of Idaho within its walls, and as he crossed the brightly polished tiled floor to the baggage claim area, he paused a moment before joining the mass of passengers waiting around the shiny carousels. Everything around him seemed highly polished, the windows letting in as much of the outside light as they could. There were patches of pure blue among the scattered clouds, and Scott wished he was in a place that had weather as good as this but without the humidity.

He started through the crowd, working his way to the edge near the front windows, where he spotted a woman in a blue suit and white blouse holding up a sign. His name was written on it in black marker.

Stiletto examined her as he approached. Her hair was down to her shoulders, but there was no mistaking her face, and the mole on her left cheek. Hollie Wilder. He'd studied her file enough to recognize her.

"You're my ride," Stiletto said.

It was the first part of a contact phrase that the woman needed to complete. Stiletto was surprised to see that she was as tall as he was.

"But it's a little rough going into the hills," she said.

"Scott."

"Hollie."

"Lead the way, please."

She turned, and Stiletto followed her out into the thick afternoon air.

CHAPTER THIRTY-THREE

Hollie Wilder followed the exit road off the airport property and onto Avenide EL Dorado and immediately pressed the brake pedal because of stopped traffic.

"Probably an accident," she said.

"Then we'll have plenty of time to talk."

"Are you here to replace Chapman?"

Stiletto blinked in surprise. That wasn't what he'd expected.

"Why do you think so?" he said. "I'm not aware Chapman is a problem."

"Then why are you here?"

"Backup and support."

"One guy?"

"Yeah."

"Seriously? Only you?"

"You'd be surprised what I'm capable of."

"I don't doubt it," she said with a short laugh, "but you don't know what we're up against."

"All I know is what HQ told me."

"They aren't telling you the whole story."

"Let's hear it from you, Hollie."

Traffic inched forward a little. She cranked up the air conditioning an extra notch.

"Chapman is either incompetent or stupid," Hollie said. "A lot of our missions have been scrubbed for one reason or another, which is frustrating enough, because if we aren't here to kick drug thug *ass* what are we doing here, right?"

"It's a fair question," Stiletto agreed.

"What's worse is some of the guys we have hit. Did you know that two of our last targets were actually rivals of the Noguera Cartel? Not even who we're here to take down."

"How did you determine that?"

"Newspapers were all over the shootings," she said. "The murder rate is actually going down in this country, if you can believe that. Suddenly we hit a bunch of guys, and the media starts asking why shootings are happening in public once again, and the politicians are freaking out because they made deals for ceasefires. We staged the hits to look like a rival cartel was targeting Noguera, thinking he might start fighting his enemies, only we didn't realize we actually *were* hitting the rival cartel, and Noguera wouldn't be affected at all. It helps him same as the cancelled hits have helped him in one way or another. It's a mess here, Scott."

Stiletto said, "None of this came up in my briefing."

"Which means Chapman isn't telling General Ike anything at all," she said. "He's running this operation according to his own agenda. He's acting as if we are still on a stand-down order while sending us here and there to do Noguera's dirty work."

"This is a serious charge, Hollie."

"How else do you explain the disaster that happened when CIA ran the op? It's no coincidence that the problems continued. General Ike brought as many of us over as he could from the CIA mission to this one. I understand it made sense because we were already here and it was better than starting fresh, but it was a horrible mistake."

Stiletto took a deep breath and looked out the window at the slowly passing scenery. Traffic was still jammed but they were getting closer to an accident ahead. Police emergency lights flashed in the daytime sun.

"He didn't realize the problem was coming from the strike team," Stiletto said.

"From where then?"

"Inside Noguera's group." *That's a lousy explanation.* "Or something," he added. *I'm making very poor excuses for the boss.*

"That's because General Ike is getting old and shouldn't be doing this kind of work anymore. He can't admit where the problem truly is coming from, which means the CIA was right to sack him and the Trust was nuts to have hired him."

Stiletto had to admit it took the threat on his wife to get the General to admit the mole might be closer to home than they realized, but he didn't say anything to Hollie.

He said instead, "Don't talk about the boss that way."

"I'm sorry, but I'm tired of feeling like I have a target on my back put there by our own people."

"Why haven't you or anybody else gone around Chapman to report to HQ?"

"Without hard evidence? We can't prove anything."

"And?" Stiletto said.

"Well, what if we're wrong?"

"But you seem convinced."

"Because we don't see any other options. It's sure as hell not *me* sabotaging the mission."

"Why did you think I was here to replace Chapman if HQ doesn't know what's really going on down here? According to General Ike, everybody is standing down until further notice."

She scoffed. "I was hoping *somebody* had discovered the problem. Why *are* you here?"

"What do you think?"

"If not to replace Chapman, I can only guess you're here to revive the mission."

"Something like that," Stiletto said.

"Except you're wasting your time. We have a bigger problem to solve first."

Stiletto shifted in his seat and remained quiet. Hollie Wilder didn't add anything more to the conversation as she negotiated a lane change to avoid the lanes blocked by the crash. A truck and a small car had collided, the car somehow ending up under the back end of the SUV, with the rear of the SUV resting on the hood of the car. The car's front end was crushed. The back of the SUV had sustained a major impact as well, the back heavily dented. An ambulance sat in front of both cars, and police were checking people sitting on the side of the road. It didn't appear to be a fatal crash, which somehow relieved Scott.

When they finally cleared the two-car wreck, Hollie Wilder pressed the accelerator, and the car picked up speed.

"Where are we going?" Stiletto said.

"You get one night in a hotel before we hit the camp," she said.

"Shouldn't we go to the camp now?"

"Can't off-road in this car."

The car wasn't very comfortable, either. An extended period in the vehicle wasn't something Stiletto wanted to contemplate.

"We'll be picked up in a Land Rover tomorrow morning, early, before traffic gets heavy. Won't take more than a couple of hours to get where we're going."

Stiletto said okay and adjusted the seat back so it reclined a little. He didn't like the delay. He wanted to get to business straight away. But he was also at the mercy of the team in-country, so there was little sense in arguing. Plus, who knew when he'd have a real bed to sleep in over the next week or two? Might as well take advantage of the opportunity.

Hollie Wilder didn't say anything more as she turned off the freeway and headed for the hotel.

Stiletto considered her statement about General Ike. Was he no longer useful in his role? How come it had taken so long for him to realize the problem was with the strike team? Why bring everybody over from the CIA job if there was a leak in the plumbing? Had the Senate Intelligence Committee actually been correct in forcing him out of the Agency?

Scott didn't want to think General Ike was getting soft and unable to perform the required tasks any longer. After all Scott had been through, lost, and all he'd regained since joining the Trust, it would be too hard a blow to handle.

CHAPTER THIRTY-FOUR

Stiletto entered the hotel room, kicking the door shut, and placed his bags on the bed. The drapes were open; he quickly pulled them shut, then rummaged through one pack to find the secure cell phone in the X-ray proof bottom. Stiletto dialed the General's number and turned on lights around the room. A little sunlight blazed through the small gap in the drapes, but not enough to light the room.

General Ike answered without saying hello. "Have you arrived?"

"Overnight hotel in Bogota until tomorrow morning," Stiletto said, and launched into his report on what Hollie Wilder had told him. He left nothing out, having repeated the information in his mind several times during the quiet moments of the drive to the hotel.

"The team has been on stand-by until we sorted the Rockwell issue," Fleming said, "and I've not changed the order. There have been no targets authorized."

"I thought so. You'd have told me."

The General said nothing.

"What do you want me to do, sir?"

"Stay the course. I'm not going to call Chapman and ask him anything. I want you to handle that."

"Okay."

"What I want is everything you can get me on the targets in question. Identities, locations, time of the action."

"What if they're playing games? Hollie is on our suspect list."

"That's for you to discover as well, Scott."

"How's your wife?"

"We're moving her tonight. There's been no sign of any surveillance activity on the base, but I'm not taking chances."

"I know the line is scrambled but don't tell me where."

"Of course. Beth will stay with her with Greg and Mitch rotating guard."

"Good luck."

"You too."

Stiletto ended the call. He took out clothes for the next day and left the rest of the gear at the foot of the dresser. There was no sense in unpacking, no need for hardware. He wasn't leaving the room. He stretched out on the bed for a nap, but Hollie's words about General Ike continued bouncing around in his head.

After an hour in the Land Rover, going uphill, the driver stopped and told Stiletto and Hollie it was time to get out the guns.

Stiletto, in the back seat, frowned at Hollie, who sat next to him.

"Hostile territory from this point forward," she said.

"I thought the whole area was hostile."

She laughed and opened her door to go around the back of the car. The driver already had an automatic weapon mounted between the driver and passenger seats.

Stiletto stepped out of the Land Rover and into soft dirt. They were traveling along a dirt road up into the hills, but runoff from somewhere made the dirt extra soft, and muddy beneath the Rover. As he moved to the back of the vehicle, his boots sank into the mud with a squish.

He was already sweating, a bandana tied around his head, his green T-shirt a little wet, his combat fatigue pants so far holding up.

Hollie removed from her pack a new Kalashnikov variant, the Ak-12. Stiletto was familiar with the weapon and complimented her choice. From his own gear back, Scott strapped on his Colt Combat Government .45 and grabbed a new weapon he was trying out. The Galil ACE SBR looked no bigger than a submachine gun, but packed the potent 5.56mm NATO cartridge in 30-round magazines of which Stiletto had a healthy supply. The collapsible stock helped make the weapon concealable under a long coat. Stiletto secured the Galil to his body with a shoulder strap, tucking the weapon under his right arm, and rejoined Hollie in the Land Rover.

"Lots of ambushes through here?" Stiletto said.

"A few."

Stiletto turned his attention to the passing scenery. It was green. Lots and lots of green. Big green leaves, thick tree trunks. If he was a vegetarian, the jungle might look like a giant salad in need of only a dash of oil and vinegar.

He cracked his window a little to better hear anything untoward should the ungodly decide to show up. The Rover's motor made a good racket, so the effort was probably useless. The air was thick, but at least the sky above the treetops was still blue.

"Up to date on your shots?" Hollie said.

"Yeah."

"Good. Lead poisoning is bad enough, you don't need malaria too."

"I don't plan on getting lead poisoning, Hollie."

"You never know."

He looked at her. "Sixth sense?"

"I've been here almost a year. Lots of lead poisoning going around."

"How many people have we lost?"

"Three."

"Because of what Chapman's doing?"

Her face remained stoic as she looked out the window. "I don't think it would have mattered."

Stiletto checked the Galil to make sure the safety was

off. Keeping the switch in the Fire position might not have been text book gun safety, but Stiletto didn't know what to expect. The Noguera cartel was a threat, obviously, but Stiletto was being escorted into a camp with at least three suspects within the group, one of whom might have betrayed the entire operation and put General Ike's wife in danger.

He might not be able to afford the extra second required to flip a safety switch. Better to be ready for anything.

CHAPTER THIRTY-FIVE

The Land Rover continued up an incline for what seemed like forever, Stiletto very glad the trail wasn't blocked by any fallen trees, though some big branches did litter the way now and then but the Rover easily rolled over those minor obstacles.

The off-road vehicle finally stopped in a small clearing, with a little overgrowth here and there, and several large tents lined side by side.

"You'll have your own tent," Hollie said as the driver applied the parking brake. "There's no room for you in the others."

"Fair enough."

Members of the strike force milled around as Stiletto exited, slinging the Galil, and collected his gear from the back. He stayed behind Hollie as they approached the group. Scott noted the Rover's driver, automatic rifle in hand, stayed behind them both. Nobody was sure of the new arrival. Stiletto didn't mind. He'd be on guard too.

"He's one of ours," Hollie announced. But that did little to smooth over the hardened faces looking Stiletto's way. He recognized battle wary warriors when he saw them, and this crew had that in spades. Their uniform fatigues were sharp, though. It was a disciplined group. No sloppiness evident. Weapons in view looked well-maintained, but Stiletto would have expected that.

Flies were ever present, but Scott spotted insect-repelled candles positioned at various points around the camp. None of the candles sat on the ground, but on logs or makeshift structure, and he questioned the use of open flame in the jungle. But it wasn't his team. He figured they were careful enough, and the foliage wet enough, so that they didn't spark an inferno. It wasn't the kind of complication they needed when the mission was tough enough already.

A tall man with shaggy blonde hair broke through the line of troops and approached Stiletto with an extended hand.

"Don't mind the frosty reception," he said. "It's been a rough couple of months."

"I understand."

"I'm Chapman. Tim Chapman."

"Stiletto."

They shook hands. Chapman had a solid grip. He introduced Stiletto to the rest of the team, but Scott noted nobody named Ben Monaghan, the third suspect on his list, was present.

"You're missing one," Stiletto said. "Monaghan."

"You're well informed. He's out checking on some things."

"Like?"

"Stuff you're going to need to see later."

He dismissed the crew, and they filtered away to whatever they were involved with when Stiletto arrived. Hollie went her own way as well. Chapman told Stiletto to follow him, and they stepped into a large command tent filled with tables and computer equipment.

"You can set your kit there," Chapman said, pointing to a corner. Stiletto complied but kept the Galil ACE handy.

"Want some coffee?"

"Tea would be better."

"I can do tea."

Chapman used a hot plate to brew bottled water and shortly presented Stiletto with a tin cup of black tea. They settled on some chairs, Chapman clearing papers from the table, and poured some packaged creamer into his coffee.

"We've been roughing it for a while," Chapman said, "waiting for base to rev up the mission again."

"That's partly why I'm here."

"I'm aware of why you're here." Chapman snapped a knowing look at Scott.

Stiletto noted his eyes didn't seem as dull as they had in the file photos HQ had provided. Had he been wrong about the man?

"Why don't you explain it to me," Stiletto said. He

drank some tea. It was hot and strong.

"I know there's a mole in the camp," Chapman said. He kept his voice low. "That's why we've been shuttered."

"Okay."

"I haven't been able to smoke out the rat. We need to be active for me to do that. You know, feed some information, real or not, see where it goes, that sort of things."

"Uh-huh."

"My money's on Monaghan."

"Why?"

"Newest member of the team. Nobody's worked with him before."

"Wasn't he with you when CIA ran this job?"

"Who told you that?"

Stiletto raised an eyebrow. "It's in the file, Chapman."

"He was a late arrival. The problems didn't start until he showed up."

Stiletto nodded. "Yet you've sent him on some sort of recon?"

"He's looking at a new processing plant the Noguera cartel started after we blew up one of their other ones."

"And how will you know if the enemy finds out we know of this place?"

"My informants will tell me."

"The same informants HQ is relying on?"

"No, my own."

"Uh-huh."

"You don't sound like you believe me."

"Mr. Chapman, all I know is that the cartel has managed to identify and carry out surveillance on General Fleming's wife."

"I didn't know that."

"This goes a little deeper than wrecking the operation locally."

"Sounds like it."

"We're looking at anybody who knew the General from his CIA days." Stiletto watched Chapman over the rim of his cup.

Chapman blinked but showed no other reaction. "That could be me," he said, "or Hollie, or Ben, or any of the others."

"Which of the others?"

"Everybody in this group worked for Special Activities at one point," Chapman said.

"Then the whole team is compromised," Stiletto said. "I'm going to report back that you all should be disbanded and replaced."

Chapman shrugged. "That might solve the problem."

"But there's another problem."

"What?"

"I want the son of bitch who's threatening my friend," Stiletto said. "He needs to be taught a lesson."

"Maybe I can help."

"Sure. Right now, I need to find my tent and get some other information from you."

"What do you need?"

Stiletto paused. Hollie had stated Chapman had sent the team to hit targets despite the stand-down order; Chapman, referencing the order, would deny any activity had taken place. Yet Scott needed the information on those unauthorized hits. He said, "Hit any targets in spite of the stand-down order?"

"No."

Stiletto nodded. He watched Chapman's face. He couldn't spot any deception.

"Okay. How are we fixed for security here?"

Chapman said, "That's one of the reasons we're so far out in the boonies. We have electronic sensors wired around the perimeter, along with some of the usual boobytraps. Two-man patrols to check on those things twice a day."

"The cartel hasn't found you?"

"They're looking. I know that. But they aren't looking in the right place."

"All right," Stiletto said. "There's a second part to my mission."

"What is it?"

"Noguera. I need to see his compound or wherever he lives. He's expecting two Americans who might be here already. They're negotiating a deal to help Noguera bring drugs into the east coast."

"I haven't heard about any visits, but I can check."

"How hard is it to get there?"

"We're actually close, maybe an hour away. By design, of course. Short drive, then hike the remainder of the way."

"Good," Stiletto said. "I could use the exercise."

Stiletto finished his tea and Chapman showed him to his tent.

CHAPTER THIRTY-SIX

The tent was a small individual camping tent with enough room for Stiletto's gear and a sleeping bag. Chapman left Stiletto to sort his equipment. The sleeping bag was plush, and looked clean, but Stiletto turned it inside out to shake away any critters who might have crawled inside. None fell out. Resetting the bag, he turned to his gear.

He ignored the bag with his clothes. The second bag held spare ammunition, body armor, grenades, and other implements he'd need in the field. He pulled out a small laptop and a satellite phone. He didn't want to try calling base with so many other team members in earshot, so he'd have to find a moment to slip away and make contact with General Ike.

He sat on the sleeping bag and looked out. The surrounding jungle felt like a cocoon. But it would be very dangerous to think they were safe within the confines of that cocoon.

Hollie suspected Chapman; Chapman suspected

Monaghan. Who did Monaghan suspect? Maybe Hollie? Was he sent away because Chapman, if he was the mole, feared what he might say?

Stiletto was being played. The mole knew he or she was reaching the point of discovery, and they were trying to throw him in different directions while they figured out an escape plan.

The best thing to do, Stiletto decided, was to keep up the pressure and make one of them crack and reveal themselves.

Stiletto had one primary goal. He needed to remove the threat hanging over General Ike and his wife.

To do so, he needed to wipe out the Noguera cartel and the mole who had put the Flemings in the crosshairs.

The biggest challenge was not letting his relationship with the Flemings influence his judgement. Stopping Noguera and the mole required cold calculation, not emotion. As Stiletto sat in the tent, staring into the distance, he wondered if that was asking too much this time. He'd always been able to conduct himself in such a manner before, but with General Ike it was different. When he'd been fired from the CIA, Stiletto felt like he'd let General Ike down, despite the unofficial help Fleming had provided in getting Stiletto out of Russia via his connections with the Trust.

He didn't want to disappoint General Ike again, because this time, failure might be fatal.

The insect-repellant candles had been extinguished at light's out, and as Stiletto lay in his tent, hands behind his back, unable to sleep, he heard airborne critters periodically smacking the outside of his tent as they flew around.

A whisper. "Scott?"

Hollie's voice.

Stiletto unzipped the sleeping bag and moved on hands and knees to the flap of the tent, pulling the zipper down enough to see two figures outside the tent. Hollie held a glow stick. It burned blue. The soft light highlighted her face and the face of the man with her. Stiletto noted his dark hair and red cheeks. Ben Monaghan.

"We need to talk," Hollie said.

"Not here."

"I know, come on. We have a spot picked out."

Stiletto left the Galil but strapped on his Colt .45 and exited the tent, quickly following Hollie and the other man away from the tents and deeper into the jungle. With their backs to him, Stiletto took out the .45. The safety was off, the hammer back, and a round chambered. He didn't trust either of them.

They could easily be luring him to one of the booby-traps Chapman had mentioned, most likely the usual trip-wire-grenade contraption used by small military units the world over in tropical settings.

Hollie and Monaghan stopped by a hollowed-out tree trunk surrounded by thick overgrowth. They faced Scott.

"You can put the gun away," Hollie said.

"I'll wait."

"Fine. This is Monaghan."

Stiletto shook hands with the man. "How was your recon?"

"I have plenty of pictures," the man said.

Stiletto turned to Hollie. Her face looked strange in the glow of the blue light. "Well?"

"Chapman is trying to throw you off the scent."

"How?"

"You asked him for information on those hits I told you about, right?"

"No. He said he was following the stand-down order."

"He's lying."

"Tell me something," Stiletto said. "How long was it until you knew about the cease in operations?"

"He's never told us," Hollie said. "I only found out by snooping through his tent and spotted the coms from home. When I got suspicious of our hits, I started looking around, and found the orders."

"Uh-huh." Stiletto turned to Monaghan. "I'm waiting to see the pictures from your recon."

"And while you're doing that," Monaghan said, "Chapman is going to run."

"Why are you so sure?"

"I've been watching him closer than Hollie."

"So?"

"Next time, ask him about his late-night trips away

from camp when he thinks we're all sacked out."

"He'll say he's talking to his informants."

"He doesn't have any," Monaghan said. "The only inside information we're getting is filtered through head-quarters. The informants aren't talking to us directly."

"Where do you think he's going?"

"To see Noguera," Monaghan said.

"I need something more than that," Stiletto said.

"Here." Hollie reached into the right pocket of her camouflage pants and pulled out a folded envelope. "The targets I told you about. Names, dates, their affiliations. See if what Chapman gives you matches this. And if you don't believe me, look up these killings. They're recent, within the time-frame of the stand-down order being issued, and now."

Stiletto took the envelope in his left hand. His right still held the Colt .45, the wooden grips warm in his hand.

"We need to get back," Hollie said.

Stiletto agreed. Halfway back to the camp he finally put away his pistol.

CHAPTER THIRTY-SEVEN

Stiletto zipped the front of the tent and rummaged through his gear for the laptop and satellite phone. Using a USB connector, he plugged the phone into the laptop and booted the machine. The bright screen lit the interior of the tent, and Stiletto turned down the brightness.

The satellite phone connected him to an orbiting spy satellite that allowed him to access the internet on the laptop. Holding a small flashlight in his mouth, he typed in the names provided by Hollie. Three men. All murdered recently in either Bogota or elsewhere, all allegedly part of drug syndicates that rivaled the Noguera cartel, all apparently not sanctioned by General Ike or Number One, the assassinations performed when the strike force was supposed to be on stand-down.

Stiletto let out a breath. He wasn't sure what to think about any of the information assaulting him at such an accelerated rate.

He consulted Hollie's notes.

She wrote a short paragraph about a shooting in Cali, where the team participated in a gun battle that killed three members of a junior narco group threatening to cut in on Noguera business. The killings sparked a series of murders as members of the group vied for further control before survivors were arrested. Noguera's business was unaffected; in fact, he absorbed the remaining members of the junior narco group and folded them into his organization, expanding his reach.

The next page detailed a series of hits carried out in multiple locations on the same day. Freelance *sicarios* were shot, mostly in public, all of whom, Hollie said, were owed money by Noguera for several killings.

The final notation described killing a woman with a car bomb. A female politician in Suarez. She'd advocated for more military use against cartels, naming Noguera specifically as a menace to the country. *This was our final straw,* Hollie noted. *This is when we realized Chapman was doing Noguera's bidding and lying to us.*

Stiletto typed the woman's name into the search bar, and read two newspaper stories about the murder and the woman's effort to clean up remaining cartel activity despite cartel "ceasefires" negotiated by other Colombian officials. She claimed they were still taking bribes and allowing cartel business to continue in exchange for fewer public shootings, but the cartels still thrives. Innocent people still suffered. The drug problem remained. Oppressors ran free while there was nobody to defend those caught in the crossfire.

Hollie seemed to be telling the truth. Unless everything she told him was an elaborate ruse to frame Chapman.

Stiletto let out a sigh. He didn't know what to think. The truth was somewhere in the mess. But how far down the rabbit hole was he required to go before discovering who was lying, and who wasn't?

He wrote a report to General Ike and emailed it to HQ. He'd have to skip a phone call. Whoever the mole was, Chapman, Hollie, or Monaghan, would keep an eye on Scott, which meant slipping away to use the sat phone posed a danger Stiletto didn't need. Better to keep the communication with base as quiet as possible. He had to assume he had no friends in the camp. His weapons would remain handy, and off-safe.

He added a personal note at the end of the report.

"Sir, I suggest we disband this strike team and start over, when the time is right, with new people. This operation is entirely compromised."

Stiletto paused and read the words. They didn't sound too harsh, which is what he wanted to avoid. He still had contacts in the mercenary community where, if necessary, he could assemble his own unit, and finish the job properly. He added that. He didn't want to sound like he was suggesting Fleming step down. Any statement along those lines needed to be consciously avoided.

If that were to come up, Stiletto wanted to say the words to the General face to face. The boss deserved that much.

With the report completed, he turned off his equipment and climbed into the sleeping bag with the .45 still on his hip and the Galil ACE within reach. He was in the middle of a den of vipers.

As he dozed off, he listened to more insects bumping into his tent. He hoped he didn't wake up to find any critters inside or, worse, hiding within his boots.

CHAPTER THIRTY-EIGHT

While the rest of the camp slept, Tim Chapman was wide awake. When his watch finally showed 0330 hours, he carefully pulled his legs out of the sleeping bag and rolled off the cot on which he lay and stood. He was still in his fatigues, his T-shirt wet from too much sweating, and he poured water from a canteen onto a rag and wiped his face. He had a quick errand to run, and he had to hurry. There wasn't much time. And he wasn't looking forward at all to driving in the dark.

He'd made the trip several times already under similar conditions, so this wouldn't be the first time.

He left the camp on foot heading south. The night vision goggles over his eyes, with the help of starlight and the blazing moon above, gave him some visibility, albeit still compromised because the canopy of trees overhead blocked most of what little light was available. But he moved steadily, slowly, along a pathway, his boots sinking into the soft ground, brushing against ground-level leaves and forcing nearby insects to silence.

He followed the sloping ground, stepping over various obstacles, finally reaching a small cave. He dropped over the top of the cave and slipped inside, where he tossed a tarp off an ATV. He mounted the four-wheel machine and started the motor. He headed east now. His destination was approximately thirty minutes away, the terrain much better thanks to large vehicle traffic having cleared a path. Chapman kept his speed low, moving his head back and forth to compensate for his lack of a peripheral view while wearing the night vision goggles.

He bounced over the dirt path but the ATV's suspension handled the terrain well. He knew it was late, way late, but nobody refused Amadis Noguera when the cartel boss demanded a meeting. Chapman wouldn't have risked leaving camp otherwise. He was sure Stiletto was aware of his movements. There was no other reason to explain his presence. He was blown. The only question now was how to deal with the situation. No matter how it ended, Chapman needed to maintain his ability to breathe.

He'd sent Noguera an encrypted message via computer advising him of Stiletto's arrival, and Noguera had responded with, "Come and see me. 4 a.m." Chapman wondered why a face to face was so important.

Chapman presently turned off the dirt path and onto a paved road, which only existed because Noguera wanted it, and Chapman increased speed as the twists and turns brought him closer to the Noguera estate. He'd only seen it in daylight once, during a recon required to show his team the enemy HQ, and it was impressive. The main house was huge, with marble columns across the front, the structure echoing ancient Greek architecture. The thick jungle surrounding it hid most of the other features on the grounds, but Chapman had glimpsed some of them on his last nighttime visit. Noguera liked gazebos, and white marble statues, preferably half-naked female statues.

The road ended at a guard shack and steel gate. The guard stepped out with his Kalashnikov leveled at Chapman.

Chapman pulled the night vision goggles from his face, stopping on command, about twenty feet from the shack. Two more troops, one on either side of the road, emerged from the foliage and one shined a light in his face. He winced.

"It's late," the guard who held the flashlight said. Chapman could not make out his face behind the bright light. "The boss is sleeping."

"The boss called me. He told me to be here. If you make me late, he'll cut your tongue out."

The guard laughed. The flashlight went out and the guard put it back on his belt. He took out a hand-held radio and spoke rapidly into the mouthpiece, listened to the crystal-clear response, and then said, "You may enter. Humberto will be waiting for you."

The two troopers withdrew and the man at the guard shack shouldered his weapon, stepping back inside the shack to activate the motor that slid the gate open. Chapman put the night vision goggles back on. The ATV rumbled as Chapman twisted the throttle, and he drove onto the property.

He followed the paved driveway to the front of the main house. The grounds around the path were only slightly overgrown, Noguera's landscapers working full time to keep the jungle from reclaiming the property.

The chief of the house guard, Humberto, a submachine gun dangling under his right arm via a sling, waited on the front steps. The low lights around the building highlighted Humberto's face. Chapman noted he did not look happy.

Chapman stopped the ATV at the foot of the steps and climbed off, removing the night vision goggles. He placed them on the seat.

"I do not understand," Humberto said as Chapman approached, "why we must meet at this time."

"Best time for me to get away."

"It is not the best time for *me*, Senior Chapman."

"Need your beauty sleep?"

"Getting old is not for sissies."

"Tell me about it."

Humberto turned and Chapman followed him into the house.

Amadis Noguera waited in the lounge, the screen up to block out the nighttime critters. He looked into the night, his back to the doorway as Humberto and Chapman entered. Chapman frowned at his bathrobe. It looked like pure silk, blue in color, with a purple abstract design weaving around front and back.

Humberto said, "Chapman is here as requested."

Noguera turned from the view. "Get the others."

Humberto nodded and exited the room.

"Others?" Chapman said.

"The mercenaries we'll be working with."

Chapman wanted more information, but Noguera stopped talking, and he knew better than to ask. He'd learn everything soon enough. He might even learn something he could use as leverage to make sure Noguera couldn't switch him off; or, rather, have Humberto or one of the other troops switch him off.

When you're playing both ends against the middle, it was best to keep bases covered.

Humberto returned. There were two men with him. Chapman recognized one of them.

CHAPTER THIRTY-NINE

"You again," said the white-haired Edward Kasson.

"I remember you too, Eddie," Chapman said.

"Explain this," Noguera ordered.

Kasson started. "I've worked with Chapman before. Angola?"

"And Libya," Chapman said.

"Is this going to be a problem?" Noguera said. He stood off to the side, looking between the two men.

Chapman and Kasson watched each other. They weren't enemies, but they had different styles of accomplishing a goal, and had come into conflict over those differing points of view often.

"I'm cool," Chapman said.

"He does what he says, and he does it well," Kasson added, "even though I think he could do better."

"Fine, then," Noguera said. "We're going to sit down, and listen to Chapman's report. That's the reason we're here."

Chapman eyed Perry Ross as he and Kasson walked by. He didn't know the other man, but could tell he wasn't familiar with combat. His face was too soft.

Noguera, Chapman, Kasson and Ross sat on the couches in the sunken center of the lounge, facing each other in a semi-circle. Humberto remained standing by the door.

"Start," Noguera said.

"The Trust sent somebody to the camp," Chapman said, and began describing Stiletto's arrival.

"Does he know you're a rat?" Noguera said.

Chapman winced at the word. "If he did, I wouldn't have survived this long. He says he's here to kick-start our operation."

"He knows about the phony processing plant?"

"I had one of my other people check it out prior to Stiletto's arrival," Chapman said.

"Make sure he finds his way there. I'll make sure my people keep him from finding his way *out* of there."

"I will."

Kasson said, "Killing one man won't get this group off your back. What's the big picture?"

"I provided the location of their base in the US," Chapman said. "A retaliatory strike will steer them off course."

"For how long?" Noguera said. "When they connect the attack to me, I won't ever be able to stop looking over my shoulder."

Chapman laughed. "Isn't that normal anyway?"

"I don't think that's funny," Noguera said. "But, yes.

You are right. Perhaps a strike on that base will do some good, even if temporarily. At least it will show them that I can get to them the same way they got to me."

"Wipe out the command and control," Chapman said, "and they'll need months to recover."

Noguera nodded. "Thanks to my sister leaving her crap laying around for anybody to find, they discovered we had the wife of the base commander under surveillance."

"I'm not aware of where she might have been taken."

"Probably the base," Kasson said. "What's the security like?"

"Heavy," Chapman said. "Contractors."

Kasson nodded. "It's a safe spot as long as they don't discover you know where they're hiding."

"We'll make an attack plan," Noguera said, "as soon as this *Stiletto* is dealt with." To Chapman he said, "Send him and some others to the phony processing plant, and my men there will be ready. Once that is done, you'll be paid and I expect you to scoot to a more genial climate than here."

Chapman nodded. He had a plan, a place to hide out, as long as Noguera didn't simply kill him. It was certainly within the realm of possibility.

He and Noguera watched each other a moment, then the cartel boss looked at Kasson.

"Will you lead the attack?"

Chapman looked at Kasson for his answer, and the white-haired man hesitated. He grinned a little. *Not so eager to fight now, old timer?*

"I can if there's nobody else," Kasson said. "Otherwise I can assemble some guys for you that will do the job."

"Good," Noguera said. "Start making calls."

Kasson looked relieved. Chapman frowned. Was he hoping for a cushy job or something? The other man, Ross, also looked grateful to have dodged a bullet. The two men had their own agenda, and Chapman wondered what it was, but only out of curiosity. His first priority was escaping with his skin intact. Because if Noguera didn't kill him, Scott Stiletto very well might.

After the meeting, Amadis Noguera eased back into his big soft bed with a sigh. Currently between girlfriends, he was sleeping alone, but that was okay, because cartel kingpins deserved to sleep alone in big soft beds with silk sheets and fluffy pillows and he'd fight to the death anybody who wanted to take that away, or take them with him in a furious blast of vengeance that even God would notice.

As he rolled onto his side, he chuckled a little. If Tim Chapman thought he was going to live to spend the money Noguera had paid him, the American had bargained wrong. When the other American, the one with the name that made him sound like a stripper's shoes, was taken out, he'd instruct his shooters to do the same with Chapman. In fact, the whole bunch of them needed to go, why was he playing with individual names? Cartel kingpins were supposed to be decisive.

And then Noguera realized that *stiletto* was also the name of a sharp stabbing instrument with a tapered blade used by a very famous mafia assassin whom Noguera admired. Perhaps the American wasn't to be trifled with.

So, yeah, they all had to go. He'd wait for Chapman to send people to the phony processing plant to be wiped out, ambushed before they arrived, and at the same time send a squad to the camp to take out everybody else. Problem solved, and Chapman could be disposed of with the rest.

And then he'd turn his attention to the United States headquarters of the Trust, and teach that puny organization that the worst mistake they ever made was taking on the Noguera Cartel. He and his sister could begin planning after he woke up.

CHAPTER FORTY

Stiletto awoke with the camp's morning sounds muted but audible. He rolled over on his sleeping bag and turned on the laptop. Plugging in the sat phone, he checked for a reply from General Ike.

The boss had responded promptly.

These were not authorized targets, and Records indicates they are indeed recent kills. See no reason to disbelieve Hollie Wilder. Has Chapman provided any other information? Suggest we move on Chapman before proceeding further

Stiletto replied:

WILL FIND APPROPRIATE TIME TO DEAL WITH PROBLEM.

He sent the message.

Then he exited the tent to find a latrine.

Hollie intercepted him as he looked through the camp and escorted Stiletto to the appropriate location so he didn't wander off and detonate a security trap.

How nice of her.

Breakfast was hot but simple, scrambled eggs and bacon pieces, along with the usual instant coffee in dented canteen cups that had seen better days but still held up to the punishment dished out in the field.

Hollie and Monaghan sat with Stiletto on the ground outside Scott's tent. As they ate, Scott noticed Chapman had his breakfast alone in his tent while working busily at the table. His laptop screen glared brightly.

"He wants to see us after we're done," Hollie said.

"About what?" Stiletto swallowed some scrambled eggs. They were liquified army eggs, from a carton, and didn't have the same consistency of real eggs, but they were still good with a dash of Tabasco sauce over the top.

Monaghan said, "He wants to go look at the processing plant I checked out."

"What was your impression?" Stiletto asked.

"Too new to be a valuable target," Monaghan said.

"A trap?"

"Probably."

Hollie shrugged.

Stiletto said, "We'll see when we get there."

Thirty minutes later, Chapman spread a paper map on the tabletop, and drew a big circle around the location of the new processing plant. He asked Monaghan to give a rundown of his visit, and show digital photographs on the laptop screen where everybody had to bunch up to see, but during his presentation he noted that he didn't think the plant was a viable target at this time, because it was too new, with no actual processing being done. It would be better to hit when the plant actually had some drugs to destroy, Monaghan added.

"Headquarters wants this place gone ASAP," Chapman said.

Stiletto and Hollie exchanged a quick glance.

"What about our stand-down order?" somebody asked.

"About to be lifted," Chapman said. "But we have permission to start with this place. And the best way, Monaghan, to keep them from refining their raw material into narcotic is to wipe out the processing plants when they pop up. So we gotta wreck this one. Keep Noguera on the run while we wait for the go ahead to attack him directly."

Stiletto returned to his tent after Chapman dismissed the team, and went through his gear. The laptop he might have to leave behind, and he set up an internal destruct sequence should somebody fail to type the correct password.

He donned his combat vest, stuffing spare magazines for his rifle and pistol in pockets, hooking grenades to loops, and strapping on a belt of six 40mm high explosive grenades. To fire the grenades, he had a H&K M320 grenade launcher. It didn't fit under the barrel of the Galil ACE, but could be used as a single-shot weapon. He strapped the M320 to his left leg with a sixth grenade in the breech and the safety off. The Colt pistol rode in a holster on his right hip.

He made sure to keep the satellite phone in his rucksack, and the rucksack on his back. He had a feeling he would need the sat phone very soon. Spare ammo, first aid equipment, and other necessities remained inside the rucksack.

He wiped his head and face and tied a bandana around his forehead. The humidity remained thick. Every move made him sweat. Out in the jungle would be worse.

Headquarters had given no such orders to hit the processing plant, Stiletto knew. And he wondered if Chapman realized he knew. The General didn't even know about the new processing plant or the reconnaissance Monaghan had carried out.

The only way to handle this was to let it play out and be ready to pop Chapman when the time came. If he survived the trap, or whatever Noguera had planned, for the group between leaving their camp and reaching the processing plant.

Chapman took the lead. He'd selected Stiletto, Hollie Wilder, Monaghan, and four other team members to go on the raid. Stiletto stayed in the rear as the squad moved in an awkward V formation through the thick vegetation. He knew Chapman was dirty, but he still wasn't sure about Hollie or Monaghan, and he didn't want anybody taking a shot at his back.

The group stayed low as the ground sloped, concealment easy in the heavy foliage, big leaves brushing at shoulders and spikey branches stabbing at necks. Insects buzzed. The air was heavy with wetness.

Stiletto kept the extended shoulder stock of the Galil ACE tucked into his shoulder, the barrel pointed down as he scanned the area, but the thick jungle gave no indication of other two-legged mammals. The bandana on his forehead was already soaked. If they stopped soon, he'd wring it out.

Chapman led the group carefully along the route indicated by Monaghan on his map, and Monaghan stayed behind to the right of Chapman with the two communicating with hand signals now and then. Hollie and the other team members remained alert, with Scott and Hollie exchanging a glance now and then in a sort of silent communication. She expected a trap; he did too. Would they have enough time to react once Chapman led them into the kill zone?

The attack came from the left.

Stiletto was looking that direction when a camouflaged gunman stepped from around a tree and raised a Kalashnikov. Stiletto shouted, "Ambush!" and dived into the vegetation ahead as the automatic weapon opened up, the chattering of that single rifle instantly joined by others to create a hailstorm of lead flying overhead, smacking into trees and ripping leaves apart.

Stiletto pushed through the foliage and returned fire, two long bursts from the Galil ACE, not identifying any specific targets, but firing for effect as he left his position at a furious knees-and-elbows crawl and found cover beside a tree trunk. He stayed low behind it as he took in the scene around him. Bits of tree bark rained down as bullets chewed through the trunk he hid behind.

The enemy force advanced with a loud scream, the strike team falling back, two dropping with holes in their upper bodies before they could get a shot off. He saw Hollie firing steady, shifting her aim and her position, as she tried to flank the ambushers. Stiletto didn't see Chapman. He looked around the other side of the tree, and still didn't see Chapman.

He left his spot and ran toward Hollie while firing, a cartel gunner dropping and another quickly taking his place. Stiletto fired again, the second gunner rolling away. Scott grabbed the H&K M320 from his left hip and fired at the closest cartel gunners. He dropped and rolled for vegetation cover before the 40mm high explosive grenade detonated.

The ground shook. Chunks of dirt and debris showered Stiletto's position. Screams filled the air. Gunfire continued in short crackling bursts, Stiletto racing to Hollie's side as she knelt over a fallen team mate. Stiletto saw right away that it was Monaghan.

"That bastard set us up!" Hollie said. She saw something, looking sharply over Stiletto shoulder. Scott pivoted to meet the threat but held back on the trigger as Chapman fired at cartel gunners, flame flashing from the muzzle of his automatic rifle. His targets went down. He stopped firing and quickly ejected the empty magazine in his weapon, grabbing another from his combat vest.

"Chapman!" Hollie took off at a run, leaping over the natural obstacles between her and Chapman, running hard at the team leader. Her M-4 dangled from her shoulder. She pulled a long-bladed knife from her belt, the sun catching on the steel blade enough to wink at Scott as he gave chase.

CHAPTER FORTY-ONE

Stiletto swung his head left and right, trying to spot any remaining threats, as he closed on Hollie, leaping over a partially hollowed-out trunk, slapping away leaves. Chapman turned to the onrushing Hollie, still loading his gun, and his mouth dropped open as she leaped for him with the knife raised for a plunge.

"Hollie!" Stiletto shouted.

She plunged the knife in Chapman's chest, to the right of his heart, and they fell together as his scream replaced any other noise. By the time Stiletto reached Hollie, she had pulled the knife out, and held it over her head for another thrust. Stiletto swung the shoulder stock of the Galil ACE against her shoulder, the impact startling her. She yelped, falling to the left, away from Scott, the knife dropping from her hand. She rolled into the vegetation.

Chapman yelled. Scott pointed the ACE at his left eye.

"I know you're the mole, Chapman!"

Chapman coughed up blood, his body convulsing.

Hollie emerged from the foliage, on hands and knees, picked up her knife, and glared at Scott.

Stiletto held out a hand to keep her back.

"What does Noguera know about headquarters, Chapman? What does he know about General Ike?"

Chapman stopped coughing long enough to smile, his mouth dripping blood. "Say good-bye to General Ike."

Chapman coughed again. Stiletto looked at Hollie. She was still on her knees, the knife clutched in her right hand, fury covering her face.

Scott stepped away and said, "Finish him."

This time, she buried the knife in Chapman's neck.

"Monaghan didn't make it," she said.

"I saw him fall." Stiletto knelt on the ground, his rucksack removed, and he unzipped the top. "We need to get back to camp and fall back to whatever recovery position you've set up."

"Come on."

"Wait." Stiletto pulled out his satellite phone and turned it on.

"We can't stay here."

"Go," he said

Hollie ran forward, Scott behind her, the Galil ACE and the HK M320 freshly loaded and ready for any attack that happened next, feeling ridiculous holding the phone as he followed Hollie's footsteps away from the ambush zone.

Not only was General Ike's wife a target, but the entire Trust complex sat in the crosshairs as well. How had they missed the surveillance? Or had Chapman provided details in person about headquarters and its security apparatus? And did he know that his information was now outdated, thanks to the increase in security troops?

"Answer me, General," Stiletto said as the phone beeped in his ear.

Finally, General Ike came on the line. "Any news?"

Stiletto fought to keep his breath as he ran, and his words came out in short bursts.

"Chapman is dead but he told Noguera about HQ and your wife and says an attack is going to happen."

"When?"

"Before I can get back. Anytime."

"Where are you now?"

Stiletto explained the ambush and that he and Hollie Wilder were heading back to the base camp. They'd need extraction. Who was in the area that might be able to help them get out of Colombia and back to the US?

General Ike said he would get going on an extraction plan. Stiletto ended the call and huffed and puffed as he ran behind Hollie, dodging obstacles, feeling his boots sink into the soft ground with every impact.

Presently Hollie held up her right hand and Stiletto stopped, Hollie dropping to one knee, Stiletto easing up beside her.

"Security perimeter?" he said.

"Yeah. We gotta go slow from here so we don't set off a bomb."

"Hollie."

"Hmm?"

"Over there. Somebody already did."

Scott pointed to two camo-clad troopers who wore the same outfits as the cartel force that had ambushed them. Scott and Hollie moved carefully toward them, weapons up and ready. The remains of an exploded Claymore mine was connected to a tree trunk, the Claymore having exploded its payload of steel balls at the two troopers and probably several others as they advanced on the strike team camp.

"We're too late," Hollie said.

They started forward again. Before they reached the camp, they smelled smoke. Once they arrived, the flaming tents and dead bodies of strike team members greeted them.

Hollie ran for Chapman's tent, Stiletto staying behind for security, but no threats were obvious. He started checking bodies. Plenty of the strike team crew had fired their weapons, and there were a few dead cartel shooters in the mix, but the cartel must have hit hard, because there were no survivors among the Trust team.

Stiletto stood in the center of the camp and felt useless. And he realized if he'd been here when the attack happened, he might have not survived either. Chapman had led them into the ambush, and had probably intended to escape when it was over, with Stiletto, Hollie, Monaghan dead, and Noguera's troops finishing off the rest. He'd expected Chapman to pull something, but hadn't thought the camp would be hit at the same time.

Maybe he and General Ike were both losing a step. Maybe it was time for both to hang up their guns.

Or maybe it was simply bad luck. Not even the strike force crew had been able to repel the attack.

Hollie called out, "Scott!"

Stiletto jogged to the command tent where Hollie stood among Chapman's gear, all of which had been trashed and turned over, computers destroyed, maps ripped in half.

"Anything still useful?"

"They wrecked it all."

"Wrecked or took?"

"Nothing's been taken. All of Chapman's computers are here, just busted. It's as if they didn't need anything because Chapman already provided it all."

Stiletto pulled the sat phone from the cargo pocket of his fatigue pants. He had to update the General right away.

CHAPTER FORTY-TWO

"Nothing left?"

"Just Hollie and me, sir."

"What about your personal gear?"

"Tent was torched."

"How can I get extraction coordinates to you?"

"GPS unit on my wrist."

"Coordinates are inbound. Start heading north of your current position, and find a safe place to turn on the machine for the rest."

"Way ahead of you. We're almost clear of the defensive perimeter now. How are things there?"

"Security force is ready, agents are armed, underground is secured. We're taking various pro-active measures as well."

"Your wife?"

"She's safe."

"I'll get there as soon as I can, sir."

"Scott?"

"Yes, sir?"

"You can't be everywhere at once."

"I understand but if I don't try, I'm going to end up putting you in the ground and I've buried enough friends."

Stiletto ended the call and stowed the phone. He and Hollie weren't running this time, but moving carefully through the vegetation, stepping over trip wires. When they finally cleared the perimeter and found an open patch of ground, Hollie stood for security while Stiletto reviewed the extraction coordinates. They started off once again.

Trust Headquarters

Isaac Fleming hadn't felt angry butterflies in his gut since his days as a Platoon Sergeant in the army, commanding a unit during Operation Desert Storm. He knew the enemy was coming. He knew the security force and available agents were capable of fighting off the invasion. But the enemy knew a lot from an inside source, which meant they might know how to access the underground command center. Fleming might have felt better if staying underground promised complete safety. It did not.

They weren't waiting idly like sitting ducks, however.

Fleming stood behind the work station of one of the command center techs, who busily worked his computer keyboard to display information on a large screen monitor on the wall ahead.

The technician, a man named Phil Gordon, spoke quickly, his hyperactive speech powered by the can of Red Bull on his desk.

"We've been digging into the background of Edward Kasson and the mercenary crews he's associated with," Gordon said, "and we're getting hits on some."

"How are you getting the hits?"

"We're monitoring the cell phones of two men specifically, and they've all received calls from Kasson to reach out to other mercs and meet at a warehouse in Baltimore."

"Are they all within the United States?"

"Only the two, sir," Gordon said. "Some have left from Europe, and we monitored those calls as well, and we're waiting for the individuals to land."

"Baltimore is only a couple hours away."

"Yes, sir."

"Who are the two?"

Fingers flew across the keyboard and three dossier photographs appeared on the right side of the wall monitor.

General Ike looked at the two hard faces on the screen, faces of men who have seen action in some of the worst of the world's hot spots. Faces of men who had killed other men up close and personal, for profit. One was young; the other, older, and sported a short beard. He didn't know their names off-hand, but Gordon filled in details.

"Tyler Kemp and Will Hanna. They're former Agency

freelancers that Kasson knew from his time there, and he's worked with them almost exclusively on other contracts around the world. CIA records show they have been very effective."

Fleming said, "Where are they congregating?"

Gordon tapped more keys and a satellite picture appeared beside the three file photographs. Fleming frowned. The structure on the screen looked like a warehouse in downtown Baltimore, as unassuming as a pair of old shoes. The parking lot in front of the warehouse appeared empty, but the satellite had captured images of two trucks parked at odd angles near the entrance. The fence around the property looked solid, and topped with barbed wire. The building might not be regularly occupied, but the owner didn't want kids throwing rocks at the windows for fun either.

"Are you sure?" the General asked.

"The warehouse is registered to Kasson, sir."

"For what use?"

"Nothing specified. But he pays the mortgage on the property. It's probably used as a staging area and storage."

"Good guess."

Fleming locked his hands behind his back and examined the warehouse picture. Perhaps the only local Noguera operatives in the area had been the ones watching his wife. Whoever they were, they weren't prepared to mount a full-scale assault on Trust headquarters. But Kasson's mercenaries were prepared, and Kasson had probably offered their services as part of his negotiations for taking over the stateside drug connection Noguera desperately required.

"Only the two so far at the warehouse?"

"Yes, sir," Gordon said.

"That might buy us some time."

"We can certainly watch them arrive and know when they leave."

"I'm thinking a pre-emptive strike."

Gordon grabbed his Red Bull and downed a gulp. "That works too, sir. But why am I telling you that?"

The General tried to smile, but his mouth decided not to cooperate. They had time. Often, that's all one required to avert a disaster. What General Ike didn't know was exactly how much time he had available before the mercenary team departed the warehouse.

CHAPTER FORTY-THREE

"It's been a long time since I addressed this many troops," General Ike said. "The last time I was leading a bunch of men your age into Kuwait."

"Oooh-rah," said somebody in the formation. Light laughter followed, but quickly faded. The team was all business once again.

The General smiled too. Young troops were always eager. Sometimes too eager. Sometimes the eager ones were the first to fall to enemy bullets. The General had written many letters home to explain those deaths; he'd taken no pleasure in doing so. The process only made the losses hurt more.

He stood on the grass near the barracks buildings, the security force, the regulars, and the back-up crew requested only a short time ago, lined up in formation. The young faces General Ike observed reminded him of every soldier he ever served with, men driven to challenge themselves and prove that they weren't sheep meant for slaughter, but warriors meant for a goal much higher than any civilian might try to reach.

"Here's what we know," the General said, and updated the team with the latest. "We don't know how many are coming. Yet. We don't know what their equipment will be. Yet. We don't know if they'll come on foot or by helicopter. All we know is that they're coming, and we need to be prepared to fight them off."

General Ike didn't mention his idea of a pre-emptive strike. He was saving that for Beth Carrington and the other operatives. If they could take out the merc team at the warehouse before they departed, there would be no need for the security force to fight, and no danger would come to headquarters personnel.

But if pre-emptive measures failed, the General needed a back-up plan. The security force *was* that back-up plan, and they needed to be fully prepared.

The command sergeant in charge of the security force, a former Marine named Max Hale, took over the briefing, dividing the force into squads and ordering a defensive perimeter line, along with instructions to get out the heavy weapons and explosives.

"We have the perimeter countermeasures that will work for us," Hale told the group. "If the tear gas doesn't disable them, the mines might do better. But we can't depend on those one-hundred percent. Some of the invaders will get through, it always happens. When they do, I want them to smash into a wall of lead like they've never seen before. That means you guys need to be on the stick and ready to defend this facility."

With that, Hale dismissed the crew, and the young men hurried to work.

General Ike turned to Hale. The command sergeant was a foot shorter, a little wider, dark-haired, with a thick neck. He was solid muscle, as his tight-fitting uniform shirt and trousers showed. He projected the aura of a man much bigger, one who had slayed his share of dragons, and wasn't afraid of slaying more. His men had nicknamed him "The Fire Hydrant", short, stocky, and unassuming, but present when required.

"What else do you need from me?"

"I need you to either get out of here or find a way to keep your head down."

The General let out a laugh. "I may be older, but I'm not useless. I'll be checking out a pistol and rifle as well."

"You're not—"

"No, but I'm not going to let anybody who gets by you put a gun to my head, either."

"What about the rest of the crew? Especially underground."

"I will ask for volunteers who can stay and help monitor the warehouse, and send everybody else home. That's my next meeting."

"Yes, sir."

"Thank you, Max."

"We haven't won anything yet."

Hale pivoted on a heel and went to join his men.

General Ike let out a sigh and returned to the main building, the peaceful-looking old Colonial house that offered no evidence of the deadly drama playing out on the surface or below.

As Fleming approached, he knew his exterior needed to be a reflection of the Colonial house. Confident. Showing no fear. The situation was under control. There would be no lives lost on compound property.

He hoped.

Colombia

Stiletto stopped and dropped to one knee. He whistled for Hollie to do the same. She complied, but glared at him.

"Why are we stopping?"

"How far is Noguera's estate from here?"

Leaving without any retaliation against the cartel leader was gnawing at Scott. He needed to strike. He needed payback. He needed Noguera in front of his gun. Taking out the cartel leader and the two American mercenaries might solve the problem, and protect General Ike and Beth Carrington and everybody else at headquarters.

"We'd have to reverse course," Hollie said. "And it would take too long on foot. We'd be exhausted by the time we got there, and who knows what we'd face?"

Stiletto looked behind them, trying to see the way

through the dense jungle vegetation. The jungle offered no help. It sat silently, save for a breeze now and then that shook the leaves, and big tree trunks having held the same spot for hundreds of years, as they would for hundreds more.

"It's not worth it, Scott."

"Dammit, Hollie."

"I get it. But now is not the time. We need to get back to headquarters and solve the problem there and then we can come back and finish off Noguera with a hell of a lot more firepower than we have now."

Stiletto turned back to her. Her intense eyes were fixed on him.

"I'm not dying in Colombia," she said.

Stiletto let out a curse. "All right," he said. He checked the coordinates on his wrist GPS, and started forward again. Hollie Wilder fell behind him.

CHAPTER FORTY-FOUR

Trust Headquarters

"Stiletto is in the air now."

General Ike stood at the head of the conference table in the underground command center. Seated around the table, as they had been before, were agents Beth Carrington, Mitch Lang, and Greg Foster.

"ETA?" Beth said.

General Ike checked his watch. "About four hours."

"What's happening at the warehouse?"

The General stepped to the side of the wall-mounted monitor and used the remote to activate the screen. The overhead satellite view of the Kasson warehouse appeared on screen. The General said, "More vehicles are out front. There were only two before, looks like five now."

"How large is the force?" asked Greg Foster.

"Our cell phone intercepts suggest at least twenty men from the US and Europe. Maybe twelve have already arrived. They could reach their full force number by the end of the day."

"What's the plan, sir?" Beth said.

"Hit the warehouse."

"Are we waiting for Scott?"

The General checked his watch again.

"He's not going to get here any faster, General," Beth pointed out.

Fleming returned his gaze to the screen. He counted the vehicles again. They had no more information than what was in front of them, and the estimate of how large a force they'd face might not be accurate.

"If we hit them now," the General said, "will the mercenaries that haven't arrived yet finish the mission?"

Mitch Lang answered. "They'll be without command and control, whoever is organizing the attack. They'll lack essential information that person probably has. Not all of them are in communication with Kasson in Colombia."

"In other words," Foster added, "they'll cut and run. Whoever is in charge of the mission is also in charge of the paychecks."

"I don't want any stragglers still hanging around," General Ike said. "Noguera will try again."

"He might try again anyway," Beth said, "until we switch him off."

"Half a threat is better than a whole threat," the General said. "At least, that's what I'm telling myself. We need to draw up an attack plan, and get ready to hit the road, with or without Scott. We'll keep an eye on the building and try to get a final tally of how many shooters are there."

"Just the three of us?" Beth said.

"No," General Ike said. "More agents are on their way. This one is all hands on deck."

By the time the other agents arrived, and were briefed by General Ike on the latest information, enough time had passed for Stiletto and Hollie Wilder to return to the US and hop another chopper from the Trust's private airstrip back to headquarters.

Stiletto felt tired all over, but there was no time for rest. He showered and shaved in his apartment while Hollie spent time with the General providing a rundown of what had been going on at the camp with Chapman, and by the time Stiletto met them in Fleming's office, even Hollie was having trouble keeping her eyes open. Beth Carrington escorted her to her own apartment to clean up, and Fleming updated Scott.

"When do we leave for the warehouse?" Stiletto said.

"What's your impression of Hollie?" the General said instead.

Stiletto blinked. He hadn't expected that. "She and Monaghan helped identify Chapman as the mole. She talked me out of doing something stupid while we were still in the jungle. I like her."

General Ike raised an eyebrow. "Something stupid?"

"I wanted to delay extraction long enough to hit Noguera's estate. She told me we didn't have enough ammo."

"And that convinced you?"

"We were a little short after the ambush, sir."

"All right. I want to keep her here for a while. See what she does."

Stiletto nodded.

"I screwed up, Scott."

"I wasn't going to say anything."

"Thank you for not disagreeing. I think." General Ike shook his head. "I missed obvious signs, I should never have brought everybody over from the CIA job, we should have started fresh."

"You were upset."

"I *was* upset," the General agreed. "I wanted to show the CIA that they had made a mistake in firing me, and in my rush, I've proved their original thesis correct. I'm too old for this."

"We aren't machines, General. We might strive for perfection but we can't always meet the standard."

"I may resign after this," the General said. "I think the Agency might have been right."

"I hope you reconsider," Stiletto said.

"No decision has been made. But I am thinking about it."

Stiletto pressed his lips together. General Ike had to make up his mind, of course, but Stiletto didn't relish the idea of a replacement. Having hoped to settle into a routine with the Trust, he wanted Fleming to be there. The General's presence reminded him that while life changes, some things don't. He wanted the familiarity, the comfort of the older man's guidance.

In the end, there might not be any other choice.

And it wouldn't be all bad. Beth was there. Number One was there, from time to time. He'd make new friends. A new family. He'd never expected to work with General Ike again, so this reunion, however short it might be, was a blessing.

"You have my support no matter what, General."

"I put my wife in danger."

"We got to her in time."

"What if we hadn't?"

"I don't know how to answer that, sir."

"There is no answer, Scott."

The two men sat in silence a moment. The General leaned back in his chair, staring past Scott. Stiletto studied General Ike's face. The worry lines were a little sharper now, the eyes tired. The General might not show it, but Scott knew he was being pushed beyond established limits. It made Scott want to strike back at Noguera as hard as possible, scorched earth, gloves off, no survivors, no mercy. Send the cartels a message that when they messed with the United States, they suffered permanent consequences.

CHAPTER FORTY-FIVE

Two panel vans sped up the interstate heading for Baltimore and the Kasson warehouse.

Stiletto rode shotgun in the lead van while Beth drove.
He was glad for the tinted windows. Anybody who
looked in and saw a man and a woman wearing combat
gear might create a problem. The back half of the van had
no windows, so the six other members of Team A rode
unobserved.

Stiletto dozed in the seat. He didn't try to keep himself
awake. The straight highway and countryside scenery
helped lull him to sleep. He needed the rest after such a
fast rush through the Colombian jungle.

The second van, with Greg Foster and Mitch Lang
up front, and six more members of Team B in the back,
followed close behind.

Each operative had a sat com unit as part of their battle
kit, with the earpiece once again nestled in Stiletto's right
ear. He was half-dozing when General Ike's voice came

through loud and clear.

"Scott."

Stiletto piped up, wide awake now. "Yes, sir."

"Get back here. They've left the warehouse."

"We can intercept them on the way."

"No. They were collected in three helicopters that landed in the parking lot in front of the warehouse. We can confirm at least twenty-five."

Beth Carrington was already changing lanes to catch the next exit and Foster and Lang acknowledged the order in Stiletto's ear as well.

"We're on our way, General," Stiletto said.

"Hurry."

The com unit fell silent once again.

Beth negotiated the exit, making a sharp left at the end of the ramp, heading straight for the on-ramp that would take them back the way they'd come.

Stiletto took deep breaths to remain calm. Headquarters was well-protected. But that didn't make him feel better. He wouldn't relax until he was on the ground fighting beside the security force, pushing back the invaders, protecting his new home, and General Ike. He wasn't going to lose either.

And heaven help Amadis Noguera if he did.

The whipping rotor blades of the ancient Huey gunship filled the passenger cabin as Tyler Kemp leaned out and examined the terrain below. Nothing but a mass of green tree tops. How much further to the target area?

He was eager for a fight.

Kemp was young enough to think of the Huey as ancient. It had probably flown in Vietnam, considering the patina on the paint outside, and the dated interior, but the machine flew and the pilots up front didn't complain too loudly and as along as the .50-caliber Browning machine gun in the left door worked as designed, they might actually pull off one of the oddest missions he'd ever been hired to carry out.

Kemp and his fellow mercs in the cabin were decked out for war, but his youthful face stood out among the hardened vets, such as Will Hanna, who was beside him. Will Hanna's partial beard was spotted with gray, his face lined, but his eyes still those of a sharpshooter.

"Where is this place?" Hanna shouted over the engine noise.

"Should be coming up," Kemp told him. They might have been father and son, having worked together so often and familiar with each other's abilities and fighting techniques, but they'd been born twenty years apart on opposite sides of the country.

They'd been key members of Edward Kasson's regular rotation for the last several years, fighting with Kasson in various world hot spots including part of Africa and the Balkans.

Kemp watched the treetops flashing beneath the chopper. They were in the first; a second Huey with another ten shooters flew behind. The third Huey didn't contain any part of the landing force. Instead, that chopper was decked out with mounted rockets and twin mini-guns to support the crew on the ground.

Kemp didn't know much about the target other than what Kasson said, that it was part of an outfit interfering with other business Kemp and Hanna might want to be a part of, and knocking out this outpost would go a long way to convincing their new employers that they should be part of the team. He'd mentioned something about big money, too, and that's all Kemp needed to hear.

"Target in sight!" the pilot shouted over the intercom, Kemp hearing the announcement over the headset.

He spoke into the microphone. "Put us down in the field."

"Copy."

The Hueys were armed with more than only the side-mounted .50-cal machine guns. Rocket pods extended from either side, mounted under short wings, and any resistance encountered as the choppers descended for landing could be handled with a burst of hellfire from the XM157 Rocket Pods and the 70mm folding-fin projectiles.

Kemp and his crew rose prepared to rappel from the chopper, hooking up their harnesses as the co-pilot triggered the rocket pod and sent two dozen flaming projectiles screaming to earth.

The small cluster of buildings in such a wide-open field made Kemp wonder exactly what was going on. It looked like a government operation, a secure base for special operators, and whoever they were, they were waiting for an attack. Stacks of tires had been strategically placed between the landing field and the buildings; defenders took cover behind the stacks, ready to shoot back. The rockets trailed smoke, heading for one of the buildings, and already bullets were peppering the Huey's outer shell.

The cabin gunner, who would remain on board the chopper, jumped behind the .50-cal and started firing, aiming for the tire stacks. The rockets landed on target, a building that looked like a Colonial home, blasting through the roof and walls and creating a blazing fireball that stretched skyward.

More return fire flashed from the tree line, Kemp and Hanna and the other mercenaries fast-roping out of the chopper to land on the airfield, immediately shooting back as they released from their rappelling harnesses, rolling flat to reduce the risk of being hit. The .50-cal thundered overhead, the chopper lifting away. The shooting from the tree line didn't last long, as the third Huey flew overhead with the twin miniguns blazing death, churning the ground into a billowing dust cloud, slicing trees and sending tree debris toppling. The Huey flew over the kill zone, circling around.

More rocket fire from the second Huey flashed, zeroing on the tire stacks. Some of the defenders ran, the rockets smacking into the ground at their heels, the explosions lifting both man and dirt into the air and back to the ground again. Kemp eyed the smashed bodies and burning tires as he and Hanna led their crew toward the flaming Colonial. They didn't know the exact size of the defending force, but their orders were to kill anybody they found. No prisoners. No survivors. When they were done, they had orders to torch the buildings. Kasson didn't want a brick left standing.

Max "Fire Hydrant" Hale let out a curse as the tree line defenders across the field were cut down in a fury of minigun fire. He didn't have a chance to catch his breath before the fighters behind the tires also met a bloody end.

"Take those choppers out!" he shouted. Two members of his squad, each braced against a tree, let shoulder-held rockets fly and speed to target, the contrails marking their launching point, but the heat-seeking capabilities of the projectiles would almost certainly find a proper home.

The first rocket struck one of the Hueys behind the cabin, the chopper exploding in midair, flaming debris falling onto the grass. The second rocket zeroed on the air support chopper, but a flare released at the last second, coupled with an evasive maneuver by the pilot, detonated the rocket before impact. The chopper turned sharply right, heading straight for Hale and his crew, and as he and his men turned small-arms fire on the canopy, Max Hale wondered if this anonymous field would be his last stand.

CHAPTER FORTY-SIX

Two more of Hale's force triggered their shoulder-fired rocket launchers and this time the projectiles scored, connecting dead center with the Huey's cabin. Hale felt the heat of the explosion as he shouted for his men to find cover, his troops dropping flat in the dense forest, flaming pieces landing all around them.

Hale looked up. There was still one chopper, with a door gunner, heading their way. Smoke filled the field, the burning tires and Colonial wreck contributing most, the wreckage of the downed choppers adding their thick contributions.

Hale shouted for his men to surge forward. The smoke would conceal them from the chopper pilot's crew, and they could engage the assault force one on one.

Hale led the charge, his men yelling as they sprinted from the tree line, the chopper passing overhead with a few useless blasts from the .50 door gun, the smoke quickly covering their movement as they sought their up-close confrontation with the invaders.

Max Hale tried not to look too closely at the bodies on the ground.

Stiletto shouted, "One minute out, General!"

"The Colonial is on fire, we've lost a lot of men, and the field is full of smoke."

"Are you secured?"

"Underground with skeleton crew."

Beth Carrington followed the access road, twisting the wheel sharply with each turn, the van's tires digging into the trail that was gratefully dry.

They cleared the access road and Beth increased speed on the approach to the compound, the air thick with smoke and the popping of automatic weapons.

"Chopper!" Beth shouted.

The Huey pilot clearly saw them, as the helicopter ceased firing on ground targets and turned to aim its bulbous nose at the arriving vans.

"Mounted rockets and door gun," Stiletto said. He had the Galil ACE cocked, safety off, in his lap. He unbuckled his seat belt and powered down the window. "Hold her steady!"

"Hold her *what*?" Beth shouted.

Stiletto pushed his upper body out the window and extended the Galil in one hand. Thirty rounds of 5.56mm weren't much against a Huey armed with rockets and a

.50-cal, but thirty rounds of 5.56mm was a lot better than throwing rocks.

The van bounced over bumps but Stiletto wasn't looking for a bulls-eye. He pulled the trigger. Flame flashed from the stubby Galil barrel. He had no idea if any of the slugs found a home. It didn't matter. Pilots aren't stupid. When somebody is shooting at them, they tend to turn their aircraft in such a direction as to avoid the gunfire.

The Huey pilot was no different, but the turn put the .50-cal door gunner in line to return fire, and just as Stiletto settled the Galil on the doorway to take a shot at the gunner, the ACE clicked dry.

Beth didn't need a warning. She was already twisting the wheel, Stiletto lurching in his seat as she took the van in a sharp left turn, the .50 hammering above, chunks of grass and dirt flying against the side of the van as the salvo strafed the ground.

"Never a dull moment," Stiletto said, snapping a fresh magazine into the Galil and smoke began overtaking the van. "Out!"

Scott and Beth pushed open their doors and jumped into the grass, the second van stopping short behind them. The back doors flung open on both vehicles, the additional Trust agents, armed to the teeth, racing into the fight.

"Who are we shooting at?" Greg Foster said in Stiletto's ear.

"Whoever's shooting at us," Stiletto said.

His eyes stung as the smoke increased and the flames

from the Colonial broke his heart. They had struck at Stiletto's new home, and there might not be a chance to save it. But he could dish out some punishment in return.

Heavy fighting lay ahead as Trust security troops tangled with the cartel assault force, Scott crashing headlong into one mercenary as he drew a knife on a Trust operative. Stiletto smashed the barrel of the Galil across his face. As the man hit the ground, Stiletto fired a burst into his chest. The salvo pinned the cartel fighter to the grass.

Stiletto turned to the Trust man. He was short. Max Hale said, "We're down but not out!"

"Lead the way!"

Max Hale and Stiletto continued on, staying low to avoid the worst of the thick smoke, shooting and moving, holding back fire when friendlies were in the way. The melee of close combat, hand to hand and muzzle to muzzle, was deafening. The smoke stung eyes and choked breathing. The enemy chopper still flew overhead, a burst from the .50 tearing chunks out of the ground now and then, but the door gunner had to avoid shooting his own people. The bursts were careful. The rotor wash did more to blow the smoke in haphazard directions more than anything.

Stiletto dropped flat as a cartel mercenary aimed at him. The salvo split the air over Scott's head, and he returned the favor with a squirt from the Galil, stitching the shooter leg to groin. The man fell screaming. Scott ran over and shot him in the head.

The intense heat from a flaming pile of tires to his left forced Stiletto to move back, coughing as smoke filled his lungs.

Stay still and you're dead.

The ancient combat adage ran through Beth Carrington's mind as she clutched her Colt M-4 and dropped flat on the grass. Shoot, roll left, shoot, roll right, stay down. She didn't bother aiming, firing only at hostiles as she saw glimpses of them, aiming for arms and legs or chests or heads, whatever presented itself. The goal was to reduce the enemy threat. Any survivors could be disposed of later.

Smoke drifted ominously, thick as the fires continued, the Colonial blaze intensifying as more of the building burned, and embers, along with bodies, landed on the grass.

She blasted the left kneecap of a cartel mercenary as he took aim at Mitch Lang, near her, and as the merc fell, a follow up burst took off a portion of his head. She rolled left, jumping up to sprint a few meters, dropped again. Movement on the right. She pivoted that way, firing full-auto, chopping down two more mercs as they ran from her muzzle flash.

Mitch's voice in her ear. "Left!"

Beth twisted her body on that direction, the sights of her rifle tracking a merc a few yards away, who was on a knee, taking aim. She fired a burst as a coughing fit seized her, the salvo missing the target. His muzzle flashed in return. Mitch screamed behind her. She didn't have a chance to look as Mitch's body landed hard beside her. She fired again, this catching the merc as he started to move. The man's ankles exploded, Beth shifting her aim as the man fell. Another follow-up burst put him down for the count.

Beth reloaded and turned to Mitch, who'd taken the enemy fire high in the chest. There was nothing she could do for him.

A flash of movement in front of her. She rolled left as automatic weapons fire tore into her former spot, smacking into Mitch Lang's corpse. A hole in the smoke gave her a perfect target, a bearded face, and her trigger finger twitched. The M-4 bucked again and the merc's head snapped back, his body covered by another wave of smoke as he fell over.

She looked around, her weapon's muzzle probing for more targets, eyes stinging from the drifting smoke, but while there were none evident around her, there was plenty of shooting nearby. Bullets zipped overhead. Her scan landed on another corpse and she sucked air sharply, coughing some more as smoke entered her lungs. *Greg!* He lay twisted on the ground. She ran to him, going flat again as she approached the body, but careful to avoid the pool of blood mixing with the grass and dirt beneath him.

Her jaw locked tight, she turned and gained her feet

again, running headlong into the battle. The smoke stung her eyes, but she had a score to settle, and she was going to make the enemy pay.

Isaac Fleming watched the fight on the wall-mounted screens beneath the surface.

He'd removed his suit coat and tie, his dress shirt, top button undone, remained, as did his pressed slacks and shined shoes. It was a lousy combat outfit, but he didn't see any other option. He had an M-4 strapped around his back.

Hollie Wilder stood nearby, in her own combat garb and weaponry. She and Fleming were the only line of defense in the underground control center, which was empty except for them and two other technicians who had volunteered to stay and help with the crisis.

He'd never felt so helpless in his life. Standing around with a rifle wearing a suit wasn't his idea of anything productive. The burning Colonial didn't concern him. His people were up on the surface, fighting and dying. He couldn't wrap his head around the probable number of casualties they might suffer, and he forced his mind to focus. This was war. He'd been to war before. But it had been a long time since he had been so close to combat.

He watched the events on screen and prayed his people could overcome the obstacles.

The heat from the flaming Colonial kept the fight away from the building, and as he wiped sweat from his face, Stiletto hoped nobody remained inside. He collided with another mercenary and dodged the swipe of the mercenary's rifle butt. Stiletto kicked him in the groin, the merc doubling over. Stiletto gave him a 5.56mm lobotomy and leaped over the man's tumbling body as he searched for another target.

He looked around but saw no Max Hale. Beth Carrington screamed behind him. Stiletto turned as a cartel gunner stuck a gun in his face. Gunfire crackled. The gunner's face vanished in a spray of red. Max Hale grabbed Stiletto's arm and pulled him away from the corpse.

Hale said, "You gotta be—"

And then a bullet smashed through Hale's left eye and tore a chunk out of his skull on exit.

As the short man fell, Stiletto raised the Galil and aimed at the shooter, a young man, who was running for the trees. Stiletto tightened on the trigger when another mercenary, a man with a beard, rolled into view, his muzzle zeroed on Scott.

Stiletto somersaulted forward as the burst flew over him, lifting the Galil to fire as a stray shot smashed into the action and sent a stinging pain up his right arm. The bearded merc took off running after the younger merc.

The remaining Huey chopper flew over, blasting smoke all around, Stiletto waving his hand frantically to clear a path as he dropped the useless Galil and ripped the Colt Combat Government from its holster.

The fighting was less now, shots sporadic, and the two runners appeared to be trying to make an escape. The chopper flew in their direction. Scott took off running, the .45 tight in his right fist, boots digging into the grass.

Shouting behind him. Scott looked back to see a Trust trooper taking a knee and lifting a rocket launcher to his shoulder. Scott dropped flat. Gunfire came his way, the two mercs laying down covering fire as the Huey descended to collect them. The Trust trooper screamed, falling back, the rocket launcher slipping from his grip. Scott fired the .45. The fat slugs didn't stop the two fleeing mercs from climbing aboard the Huey. *At least there aren't more making a run for it.* Stiletto ran to the fallen trooper's rocket launcher. A quick scan of the action showed the weapon was primed. Scott dropped the Colt and hoisted the launcher to his shoulder.

The Huey lifted away from the grass and started making a turn for the trees. Stiletto squeezed the firing button. The rocket launcher belched flame as the heat-seeking projectile left the tube.

The missile struck behind the cabin. The force of the explosion rocked the ground.

Smoke continued to drift around them, but the gunfire had finally settled down. Scott dropped the rocket launcher and picked up his pistol.

"Rally up!" Stiletto shouted. He wanted a head count

of survivors before venturing below to the underground control center where General Ike and his skeleton crew were hiding. The forest was going to burn along with the rest of the compound. He needed to know if there was a way to stop that from happening.

Stiletto wasn't sure how many of the security force was lost in the fight, but as the crew gathered away from the fires, he counted fifteen. Beth stepped up beside him. He asked where Greg and Mitch were. She shook her head. Beth had taken a bullet graze on her neck, and blood had leaked onto her left shoulder and sleeve. She shook off any help.

Putting out the fires and getting those below ground evacuated was the top priority, and the security team stepped up. There were fire hoses in the barracks build-ings, with access to water via piping from a nearby stream. While the security crew started fighting the fires, Stiletto talked to General Ike on the com unit about an alternate way to get underground. Beth answered first. A tunnel from the operatives' barracks led into the command cen-ter, and Stiletto followed her into the building, which had been damaged by stray gunfire but hadn't caught fire.

Stiletto and Beth cautiously entered the first floor of the barracks, because they didn't know if any cartel killers had taken cover within. The entryway was clear, as were the hallways to the left and right, and the area further forward which contained rows of bunks. Beth led Scott down the hallway to the left, passing shower areas and lockers, to a door without any markings on it. The doorknob had a keypad next to it, and she punched in a three-digit code. The locks snapped back.

Stiletto spoke to General Ike over the com unit, advising him that they were on their way down and that the fight was over and the fires now taking up everyone's attention. The boss acknowledged. By then, Beth and Scott were halfway down a spiral staircase and ended at another combo-locked door, where Beth pressed a six-code combo this time. The door snapped open. She entered first, Stiletto following close behind, and they ran to the General and Hollie and the two techs.

"Beth, you're hurt," the General said.

"It's nothing, sir."

"Everything okay?" Scott said.

The General assured them all was well. Scott asked if there was anybody else down there, armed, other than him and Hollie Wilder. The General said no.

"Then it's a good thing we kept them from getting down here," Scott said. "Where's your wife?"

"Safe," the General said. "But considering this compound no longer is, I suggest we get out of here as fast as we can."

Nobody argued.

"Do we have vehicles?" Stiletto said.

"Hidden in the forest," the General said.

CHAPTER FORTY-SEVEN

The security force and other agents stayed behind to continue fighting the fires, trying to keep the barracks and general quarters from burning, and chasing embers on the grass that started smaller fires. Luckily those were easier to put out. The air was still choked with smoke, and as Stiletto drove away from the compound in a supercharged Tahoe with General Ike, Hollie Wilder, and Beth Carrington, he felt conflicted. They needed to protect the principal, in this case, General Ike, but their colleagues and fellow fighters needed help at the compound too.

All Stiletto could do was keep looking forward and let other people handle their various responsibilities. He wasn't superhuman. He couldn't do everything, couldn't cover all the bases, couldn't carry the load alone. He was covered in soot and dried sweat. He felt disgusting, and could only imagine Beth felt the same. Adding to their burden were the deaths of Mitch Lang and Greg Foster. He hadn't known them well, and he was sorry for that more than anything. One should know the men he fights next to, but he hadn't had the chance. He glanced at Beth's face in the rearview mirror. She was holding together, but her eyes were wet. She'd known them longer. Stiletto let out a breath. There was nothing to do but keep moving forward.

The General had ordered the off-site stashing of several vehicles for an escape, and the two technicians who had stayed behind took one to go their own way and stand-by for news.

Fleming directed Scott to drive to Baltimore. Scott did a double take at the order. Yes, it was a long drive, but that's where Mrs. Fleming was staying, at a hotel, in a big city where there were plenty of places to hide, and he wanted to reunite with her while they contacted Number One and planned their next move.

Stiletto only had one move in mind.

Attack.

But first things first.

Secure General Ike. Get some rest. Recharge. Only then could the fight continue.

Luckily Stiletto, Beth, and Hollie wore civilian clothes under their body armor, so their weapons and other accoutrements remained in the Tahoe, properly concealed in a non-transparent equipment case in the rear of the vehicle. Beth wore the General's suit coat to conceal the blood on her clothes. Hollie had fashioned a bandage for Beth's neck from the First Aid kit during the long drive from the compound. Everybody was wiped out. The General could crash with his wife, but Stiletto and the two women were on their own. Hollie and Beth secured a room to share, while Stiletto had his own.

Scott stepped out of the hot shower and toweled off. He felt cleaner, but his body ached from lack of sleep and the strain of the last few days. He didn't bother getting dressed again. His street clothes were filthy and smelled foul. While they might survive a small amount of public exposure, the jeans and shirt were not a long-term solution even if he could get them washed. The General's idea was for Mrs. Fleming to go out the next day and acquire new clothes for everybody, including something for him. Such was the hazards of life on the run.

He wondered how things at headquarters were shaping up. Or was it now their former headquarters? The General had a scheduled call with Number One to discuss the situation. His orders for Stiletto, Hollie, and Beth, in the meantime, was to get some rest.

Stiletto fell naked onto the bed and managed to pull a sheet over him before he quickly passed out.

A knock at the door.

Stiletto awoke with a start, lay still a moment, and when he heard the knock again, grabbed the hotel bathrobe from the floor and quickly tied it on.

He opened the door. General Ike stood in the hall.

"We need to talk," the boss said.

"What time is it?" Stiletto stepped back to let Fleming enter.

"Late enough. I just finished an update with Number One."

Stiletto shut the door. All he had to offer General Ike was water from the sink. Fleming waved him off. They sat at the table by the window. Stiletto noted that Fleming was still in his suit clothes.

"We have orders to stand down," Fleming said.

"What?"

"Number One says we're officially out of action. He's going to assign a new strike force to take on Noguera. Take *out* Noguera is how I should phrase it. We're done."

"No, sir."

"We don't have a choice."

"Then I'll back to Colombia myself."

Fleming laughed. "Repeat that to yourself very slowly, Scott."

Stiletto considered the words a moment, and let out a sigh. His whole body seemed to deflate. "Noguera is our job to finish, General."

"No. He's the *Trust's* job. We're to stay behind. We have a lot of rebuilding to do."

"New headquarters?"

"The compound is untouchable right now. The fires

are out. Nobody else is hurt. But we have a lot of dead to take care of, ours and theirs, and this is going to hurt for a long time. I'm afraid we may be scattered about until further notice."

"I'm living in a hotel for a while?"

"We'll work something out."

"When is this new strike team heading out?"

"Assembling now."

"Do you have a part in it?"

"What have I just said, Scott? No. And not because I fouled up this one so bad."

"What did you tell Number One about that?"

"I have not brought up my resignation. But I have said that once this is over, he and I need to have a serious talk about my future."

"He knows what that means," Stiletto said. "The man isn't stupid."

"That's why he's the top dog." The General rose from the chair. Scott walked with him to the door. "Take it easy for a few days. I'm going to tell Beth and Hollie as well. Hollie has no reason to stay with us, so she'll be free to go."

"Heck, maybe she can put us up at her place."

The General laughed. Scott opened the door. Fleming said good-night, such as it was, and started down the hall. Stiletto watched him walk the length of the hallway to his room at the end of the hall. Scott was glad they were on the same floor in case of an emergency.

Stiletto shut the door and sat on the edge of the bed staring at the carpet. What more could he have done? Should he have remained in Colombia to hit Noguera before the attack on the compound happened?

He yawned. Exhaustion was overpowering his thought process. It was time to indeed get some rest. Stiletto had chosen a job with the greatest amount of job security ever, assuming you didn't get killed in the line of duty. There would always be another fight. There would always be another Amadis Noguera. Scott might have to sit out the final battle in this case, and maybe that was okay.

He wanted to see justice served, but he was not invincible. Fallen allies like Mitch Lang and Greg Foster and Max Hale continued to hammer that point home. It could have easily been his body lying on the grass back at HQ. Almost too easily.

CHAPTER FORTY-EIGHT

Stiletto slept well into the next afternoon. Not even dreams disturbed him. He checked in with General Ike after showering, and the General said he had some clothes for Scott, which he promptly delivered.

The General's wife had provided him with jeans and a button-down shirt and all he needed was a cowboy hat to make the look perfect.

Stiletto and Fleming didn't speak. As Fleming stood in the doorway to leave, he only nodded at Scott.

"Tell your wife thank you, sir."

The General nodded again and left without a verbal good-bye.

Scott shut the door. They were all having a hard time, and General Ike more than anybody. Scott wished he could help the man. Say something to convince him he wasn't to blame. No words came to mind.

He tried on the clothes. They fit. Mrs. Fleming had also provided a jacket, but he left that behind as he left his hotel room to get some fresh air.

Standing on the sidewalk outside the main hotel entrance, Stiletto took a deep breath and for the first time in a long time, felt free. The thought stunned him. There was no target on his back. Nobody gunning for his hide. Then he thought of others not so lucky, who hadn't survived the previous day, and his mood soured again.

He found a Walgreens down the street and picked up some pens and a notebook of blank paper. A taxi dropped him at a cigar shop, and he picked up a Montecristo and sat in the shop's lounge. As he sank into the soft leather chair, he opened the package of pens, and selected one. In the notebook he started drawing.

The last time he'd done any sketching was in Twin Falls, ages ago now, and he let his mind take over as his hand followed the directions of his subconscious. He drew a man without wings flying in the clouds, his legs tight together, his arms outstretched.

Maybe that's how he felt knowing his problems with the Russians were over. It certainly beat the alternative. When he returned to his hotel, he might even open the drapes. There wouldn't be any snipers on the roof across the street.

Unless Noguera put them there.

He paused with the pen hovering above the page. He put the pen down and sat back puffing on his cigar. The fact that nobody had found Mrs. Fleming since her placement at the hotel proved there wasn't a leak inside headquarters, but what if . . .

What if.

It was too soon to celebrate *any* sense of freedom. They truly couldn't rest until Noguera and his cartel army was smashed to pieces. He hoped the new strike team going to Colombia succeeded, otherwise they were standing at square one.

Stiletto set his cigar in the ashtray beside his chair and returned to drawing.

The General broke the news after dinner.

Fleming had asked Stiletto, Beth, and Hollie Wilder to join him and Mrs. Fleming in their suite, and room service delivered. Seating was haphazard, with holding chairs also brought up so they could sit in a group, but it still required Scott, Beth and Hollie to balance their meals on their laps while the General and his wife used the table.

Mrs. Fleming looked as haggard as the rest of them, but she wasn't complaining. If this was her first look into the danger her husband faced on a daily basis, she didn't give away her internal thoughts.

They finished and stacked the dishes outside the door and the General asked them all to gather around once again. Scott and Beth exchanged looks. The tone of his voice suggested bad news. Scott looked at Hollie, who didn't make eye contact with him. She was hanging on for the ride, not officially part of the group, but there was also nowhere else for her to go. She was as invested in Noguera's defeat as they were.

"The strike team failed the primary objective," the General said.

Beth jumped in before Stiletto could get the words out of his mouth. "What happened?"

"The raid on the Noguera estate, the attacks on processing plants and growing fields, all were successful. Noguera will not recover easily."

"He's still alive," Stiletto stated.

"Our people found no evidence of Noguera, his sister, or the two Americans, Kasson and Ross, at the estate," the General said. "There were vehicles missing from a garage, so it's assumed they evacuated prior to the attack."

"Before?" Stiletto said.

"Yes, Scott."

"Is there another leak?"

"What do you think?"

"I don't know *what* to think, sir," Stiletto said. "Other than we've lost this one. I'm not satisfied that Noguera's cartel is probably broken temporarily. As long as he's breathing, he'll rebuild."

Stiletto waited for a response. Nobody argued. All eyes were on him.

"Do we regroup and continue pursuit, or what?" Stiletto said. "Does Number One even know where to put us now?"

"We'll have a new home," the General said. "Maybe

even the old one. The Colonial can be repaired and there was very little damage to the barracks. But that's a few months away."

"I'm not sitting on my keister for a few *months*, General."

Beth said, "Neither am I."

Hollie remained quiet.

"I don't expect you to," the General said.

"Then what are we going to do?" Scott said.

"What would you do? If you were in my position, what would your idea be?"

Stiletto blinked. The General had never posed a question like that before. Was the boss giving up on himself? Was he no longer confident in his own decision making?

Scott indeed had an answer to the question. It might not be what the General would have guessed, but with Noguera and Company on the run, and no leads, there was one thread they could pull on that might turn up the entire nest of rats.

"I have one idea," Stiletto said.

"Don't be shy."

"It's a big *maybe*. It could be a dead end but it also might pan out."

"The lawyer?" Fleming said.

"No, not Rockwell. I'd like to know who took over for Giles Flynn."

Fleming blinked.

CHAPTER FORTY-NINE

Somewhere in Boston

The black gate Giles had been so proud to install in their second home swung closed, and the black Lincoln slowly eased up the very clean driveway. The centerpiece of the front yard was a perfect patch of green grass with a tall tree growing dead center. The house was not only secured by the main gate, but encircled by a wall, but the wall was almost invisible because of the other trees and multi-colored flowers blooming around the perimeter.

Giles had liked this house. He called it the Sanctuary. It was where he could sit outside, under the sun, and enjoy the chirping birds and the smell of freshly-blooming flowers.

Barbara and her daughters were staying here because somebody had blown their other house to hell and gone along with Giles.

As the black Lincoln approached the house, the vehicle

passed several armed men with rifles and shoulder-holstered handguns. She wondered what the occupants made of the sight of so many men with guns nearby, but then she decided it would be a familiar sight. She and the men inside the car weren't that different.

Barbara Flynn watched the car follow the gentle curve at the end of the driveway to come to a stop only a few feet from the porch under which she stood with folded arms and a *I told you so* smirk.

The passenger side faced her, and the back door opened and Amadis Noguera slowly eased out of the vehicle. Nobody exited with him. He left the door open, and Barbara Flynn caught a glimpse of others waiting inside.

The armed troops quietly assembled around the parked vehicle, one stepping onto the porch beside Barbara Flynn.

Noguera stopped at the foot of the porch steps without a glance at the killers waiting for an order to snuff him out. He looked good for a man who had only hours before fled Colombia with a thousand bullets fired at his back.

"I don't deserve to be here," he told her.

"Why is that?"

"I said some awful things, Mrs. Flynn."

"You meant them at the time. Are you going to tell me you didn't mean them now?"

"I meant them. Every single one. But now we need each other."

"I don't need you. The only reason you haven't been shot dead in my driveway is because it would be hell to clean up."

Noguera huffed. "You aren't going to shoot me, or my people."

"Why?"

"Because I'm bringing you a gift."

"Your hands are empty."

"I know who killed your husband."

"Really?"

"I know the man's name. I know who sent him. I can deliver them all to you."

Barbara's smirk faded. She'd been resolved to tell Noguera to drop dead. But now her mind spun with another thought. The possibility of revenge.

Unless he was playing her.

"In exchange for what?"

"What you asked for. A resumption of our deal. I have much rebuilding to do, but the drugs and money *will* flow again. You can profit from that. You can also have your revenge."

"You're lying."

"I am not."

She studied his face. He was stoic, looking directly at her. She saw desperation in his eyes. He couldn't control what was behind his eyes. But it wasn't the desperation of a man playing his last hole card. He was desperate for sure. Looking for a lifeline, yeah. But he wasn't lying about knowing who killed Giles.

"How do you know all this?" she said.

"That will have to remain my secret."

She laughed. "You got somebody on the inside."

Noguera smiled. "I have somebody on the inside. That is correct."

"Where are these people?"

"Baltimore. At a hotel. I attacked their headquarters and sent them running. They attacked my estate and sent me running. It's a never-ending cycle, Barbara."

"Don't I know it," she said. She lowered her arms. "All right. I will listen to your proposal. Bring your people inside. Is anybody armed?"

"We are not armed. You may check."

"I'll trust you. But look at the firepower around you. If you try anything—"

"My intentions are peaceful, Barbara. We both have an empire to rebuild, and we can help each other."

She wanted nothing more than to believe he held the answers she wanted, and could provide her and her daughters with satisfying vengeance. The act wouldn't bring back Giles. They were still on their own. But she might be able to sleep better at night knowing her husband's killers were six feet under. She had to remain cautious, and not look too desperate herself.

"We'll see about that," she said. "Who else is in the car?"

"My sister, my chief body guard, and two American mercenaries."

"Bring them inside."

CHAPTER FIFTY

A shrill alarm and pulsing strobe woke Stiletto with a start.

He sat up in the dark hotel room, squinting against the flashing light. *The fire alarm.* A voice over a hallway loudspeaker was audible through the closed door.

"We have a fire reported in the basement. Emergency crews have been notified. Please evacuate your rooms following the emergency plan posted in your room and do not use the elevators."

Scott threw the covers off and turned on the bedside lamp. He jumped into the clothes he'd discarded on the floor. This wasn't only a fire. The Noguera Cartel was literally trying to smoke them out. They'd caught up somehow. There was another leak. *In their group.* Stiletto had to get to Fleming and his wife and fast.

Grabbing his jacket and wallet, he made a last stop at the room's safe. The strobe continued its pulsing, but the light from the lamp lessened the effect. He ignored the alarm. Scott punched in the combination, wrenched open the door, and removed his .45 and shoulder holster. He donned his holster and jacket, and then left the room, pulling the door shut behind him.

Already other guests were rushing past him, most in night clothes or bathrobes, all panicked, all heading for the stairwell. Stiletto moved against the tide, heading in the opposite direction, toward Fleming and his wife. Scott spotted a pair of firemen at a door in that direction, and a shrill alarm of his own sounded between his ears. He started running, dodging the flow of guests which quickly dissipated, shouting, "Hey!"

One of the firemen turned his way. He wore street clothes under the fireman's coat; in other words, enough of a disguise to fool people who weren't paying attention. But not Scott. They were Noguera's men and no mistake.

The phony fireman facing Scott swung up an axe, and as Stiletto checked his speed, the man lifted the axe over his head. He brought it down in a smooth arc, the blade whispering past Stiletto's nose, the blade glancing off the carpet. Scott clapped his hands over the man's ears, the man letting out a yell, following up with a palm strike smack in the man's solar plexus.

The second fireman lunged at Scott, grabbing him around the middle and pushing him back into the hallway wall. Breath left Scott as he tried to wedge a knee between him and the other man. Then he saw two more fireman carrying Fleming and his wife out of the room, over their shoulders, both seemingly unconscious. Scott grunted as he blocked his attacker's blows. When the phony fireman stopped and pulled away, Stiletto felt a weight leave his left side. The man had his gun. The snout of the .45 rose to Stiletto's face, but the man had stepped back too hard. A solid kick into the man's groin brought him down, Stiletto grabbing the .45 and twisting the pistol free. He smashed the barrel down across the man's head, then started to run after the two who had the Flemings, but his legs wouldn't work.

The first fireman had a bear hug on his ankles, keeping his legs together, and Scott fell over like a tree.

The fire alarm, the recorded announcement, and multiple strobe lights continued in the hallway as Stiletto landed on his chest. Stunned, it took a moment for him to recover, but he held tight to the .45 as he felt the other man getting up. One kick in the ribs. Scott cried out, rolling away from the second kick, but bumping into the other wall. He blocked a third kick and then rose to a knee to jab the .45 into the man's stomach. One pull of the trigger. The alarm drowned out some of the .45's blast, but nothing stopped the explosion of red that burst from the back of the man, staining the white wall behind him. Scott shoved the body aside and was back on his feet running before the Noguera thug hit the floor.

Stiletto ran to the end of the hall. There was no sign of Fleming, Betsie, or the other two fake firemen. They'd taken the stairs down. To the lobby? To another floor?

Where? Scott crashed through the door, more guests rushing past him, some haphazardly dressed this time. The alarm was louder in the stairwell, the sound bouncing off the concrete walls to create a cacophony of ear-splitting migraine-inducing insanity. Scott stowed his gun before anybody noticed the automatic, and joined the flow, trying to peek over heads and shoulders to see ahead, but the short landings and corners prevented him from getting a view of the Noguera team.

The flow was slow and backed up when other guests from lower floors joined in, and the mass of movement and panicked voices didn't make Scott's job any easier. His cell was in the right inside pocket of the jacket, and Scott grabbed it, breaking free of the crowd through a door to a lower floor. He hurriedly punched in Beth's number, but the call went straight to voicemail. He tried Hollie Wilder's number. No answer. Had they been taken out early?

Stiletto ran to the floor's elevators, but they had been shut down. There was no way out but the stairs. He ran back to the stairwell and moved as fast as he could. He'd lost too much time already.

On the street, he pushed through the gathered crowd of guests who were looking for flames on the outside of the building but finding none. There were three fire engines in the street, perhaps genuine firemen proceeding into the basement and the blaze there, but that wasn't Stiletto's concern. He frantically looked around. Police were herding guests to the other side of yellow caution tape they'd used to block the street in front of the hotel, and Scott headed that way, jumping to see over heads, and still saw no sign of the General and his wife.

"Scott!"

A woman's voice calling from his left. Stiletto spun that way. Hollie Wilder waved from an alley. He looked around. The alley was out of sight of the activity on the street. They might be able to talk and slip away without being seen.

He ran toward Hollie, suddenly stopping short as a sight in the alley sent a chill up his back.

Beth.

On the ground beside a Dumpster.

Blood pooling under her head.

"What—"

Hollie brought up a pistol. "Barbara Flynn sends her regards." She pulled the trigger on the double-action automatic, Stiletto registering the backward movement of the hammer as he ducked under her arm. The gun barked over his head. He slammed a tightly balled fist into her stomach, ramming his head into her midsection as she doubled over, and slamming her back into the alley's brick wall.

The gun fell from her hand as he spun her around, both arms around her neck. She struggled, kicking at his shins, her arms unable to break the hold he had on her.

"Tell me where they're going and I won't snap your neck!"

"Never!"

One of her feet landed on his left shin and he grunted, his grip on her neck tightening. She yelled, the scream choked off, and Stiletto said, "One last chance."

She shouted, "Flynn's other house in Boston!"

Stiletto shoved her forward, face first into the wall, her nose snapping with an audible pop, and then her skull as he pulled her head back and shoved it forward again. He stepped back and let Hollie's body crumple onto the ground.

He ran to Beth. He examined her for wounds, but only her neck was bleeding from a re-opening of the bullet graze she'd sustained during the battle at headquarters. Otherwise she was only unconscious with one heck of a welt on her head.

He went back to Hollie and searched her for a cell phone. He found it in her back pocket. The captured phone went into his own pocket and then he picked up Beth, put her across his back, and headed for the opposite end of the alley.

Hollie had been the second leak. No wonder she hadn't wanted him to detour and take down Noguera at his estate. She'd needed to worm her way into Trust HQ and continue her effort to take down the operation from the other end. She'd fed them Chapman so they'd think he was the only one.

He'd been right about the Flynn connection. Noguera and his crew had run to her for help, and because of

Hollie, knew exactly who had killed her husband. They'd formed an alliance based on Noguera's promise to deliver Stiletto and Fleming to her doorstep.

As Beth's weight bore down on him, Stiletto decided she wasn't the only damage he'd be carrying if he failed to rescue Ike and Betsie Fleming. And he had very little to go on. *Flynn's other house in Boston* meant nothing.

CHAPTER FIFTY-ONE

Beth stirred, groaning as she put a hand to her head. "What happened?"

Stiletto had placed her on the sidewalk a block away from the hotel. They were under the front window of a music store, which displayed various instruments. Luckily the store was closed. Nobody on the sidewalk to gawk at them, either. A nearby street lamp shined over them.

Stiletto told Beth to stay quiet as he knelt beside her with Hollie's phone to his ear.

Stiletto didn't need to look too hard on Hollie's phone to find the clue he needed. One of the first numbers on the recent call list began with "57" followed by "1" and then a number. "57" was the international area code for Bogota. She'd been talking directly with Amadis Noguera.

"What is it?"

The drug cartel leader's voice came through loud and clear.

"She *missed*," Stiletto snapped.

"Who is this?"

"The man you promised to deliver *dead* to Barbara Flynn, only that isn't happening, and when she finds out you failed, your little alliance might end up in jeopardy."

"We have the other two."

"Won't be good enough for her, Amadis. You know that."

"What do you propose?"

"I'll come to you."

"To surrender?"

Stiletto laughed. "No."

"To what then? You're facing a small army here. Do you plan to come alone?"

"Why don't we let that be a surprise."

Noguera laughed. Then he stopped laughing and didn't say anything, but Stiletto heard him breathing.

"All right. You were supposed to be part of the package, too."

"Tell me where to go. We'll meet face to face very soon."

Noguera provided the house address.

Stiletto didn't need to write it down.

Scott tore fabric from the bottom part of his shirt and tied it around Beth's neck without strangling her. They had no proper first aid kit to clean and dress the wound.

"It'll have to do," he told her.

"We've both had worse."

Kneeling on the hard sidewalk as he helped her pull on her jacket to cover the neck wrap hurt his knees, but he ignored the discomfort.

"I didn't have any warning, Scott," Beth said, as Stiletto unwound some gauze. "The alarm went off, and she beaned me over the head."

"It's okay."

"Where's the General?"

"Captured. His wife, too. I couldn't get to them in time."

"What are we going to do?"

"*We* are not going to do anything, Beth. You're staying here."

"But—"

"This is my fight. You're also growing a potato on your head. You're in no shape for another battle."

She wanted to argue, but as a wave a pain passed through her, he knew she wasn't going to keep up the fight.

"Back to the hotel?" she said.

"We have our vehicle there, the gear I'll need."

"It'll be a long wait."

"We have a little time."

"Help me get up."

Stiletto stood and grabbed Beth's outstretched hand, bringing her to her feet. She leaned against him a moment to catch her breath.

"What happened to Hollie?"

"I left her in the alley. She won't bother anybody ever again. Come on."

They couldn't get back into the building for a minimum of two hours, so Stiletto and Beth found an all-night coffee shop and a table in the back. They nibbled at pastry, with black coffee for Beth and hot Earl Grey for Scott.

When the fire and police crews finally gave the all-clear, it was close to sunrise, the morning glow filling the streets as weary hotel guests moved back inside the building. Stiletto and Beth joined them and went straight to Scott's room where he called for a first aid kit and took proper care of Beth's neck wound. Then it was down to the garage to check out the supercharged Tahoe and the hidden compartment of weapons. They had to remain in the confines of the Tahoe, with its tinted windows, to go through the equipment and not be seen.

The last thing they needed was to be caught on surveillance video inspecting fully-automatic weapons.

His Galil had been destroyed in the fight at headquarters, but he had three M-4 carbines to choose from, one used by Beth, the other two by the General and Hollie. The Tahoe also still contained H&K MP7s, but those weapons had limited amounts of ammo. He had enough 5.56mm ammunition for the M-4s to fill the pouches of his combat vest and shoulder holster. He still had the H&K M320 grenade launcher and a small selection of high-explosive projectiles. He hadn't used them at the headquarters fight because of the close proximity of the fighting, but they would come in handy now.

Just like they had at Flynn's first house.

"Are you sure I can't at least help you drive?"

"I need you here. You need to update Number One. As of now, you're all that's left of our group, and if I go down, somebody needs to tell the Trust what happened."

She didn't blink at him.

"Are you considering this a suicide mission?"

"Not at all." Scott started returning the gear to the storage box. He couldn't be caught wearing combat gear. "But you never know. You can't keep up this sort of thing forever."

He still wore his shoulder harness, and covered the rig with his jacket.

He left Beth standing in the garage as he pulled out into the street. He checked the dashboard clock display. Seven a.m. The dash GPS told him his drive would last six and a half hours. Not ideal, but he had no choice. The Flemings were in danger. He needed to get them out of there and leave nothing but ashes and enemy bodies behind.

If they were still alive.

If Barbara Flynn, Amadis Noguera and his gang had already killed them, Stiletto's vengeance would be severe. No quick kills, no clean shots. He'd make them suffer as long as possible. He had to stop himself from dreaming up a variety of torture techniques. They were only making him mad, and put visions in his head he didn't want or need. Noguera and Barbara Flynn weren't going to kill anybody until Stiletto arrived. She wanted all of them in one room so she could shoot them one at a time.

She'd be disappointed.

Stiletto followed I-95 north. There were toll stops along the way, and they couldn't be avoided. He and Beth had scrounged their cash together for enough to get him through those toll spots. Nothing could slow him down.

Nothing.

CHAPTER FIFTY-TWO

Isaac Fleming woke up gagged, hands tied behind his back, ankles bound together, and jammed into a trunk.

There was another body against him. Had to be Betsie. He couldn't raise his head to see if she was conscious or not, and the darkness in the trunk would have prevented him from seeing her face anyway, but she wasn't moving or making noise, thankfully, so she was probably still out cold. Or frightened into total silence.

He rubbed the sides of his wrists together. They had used a strip of bedsheet to tie him. Why did they have to improvise? The appearance of the Noguera goons had seemed improvised from the moment they entered the hotel room "dressed" as firefighters. They weren't fooling anybody. And had Fleming been in better shape, had he not spent so many years behind a desk, he might have stood a better chance of getting Betsie out of danger.

The car jolted over bumps, Fleming hitting his head on something, grunting. No noise came from Betsie.

And that started to bother him. His pulse began to race. Was she out cold or dead?

He had to breathe through his nose, and shut his eyes tight, forcing from his mind any thoughts of her death or their impending doom. There was always a way out. As he lay there jammed into too small a space, full of stuffy air and the putrid scent of exhaust fumes, he forced his mind to stabilize.

Had Stiletto been taken? What about Beth and Hollie? They might be right behind them.

He grabbed onto the hope the thought offered as the vehicle continued rumbling along the blacktop.

The two thugs still wore their fireman coats.

Fleming would have laughed if the situation wasn't so grave.

He was coated in sweat. He hadn't realized he'd been sweating so much, but as the trunk opened and fresh air flooded into the compartment, Fleming felt the wetness on his body, and the air smelled nice compared to the stuffiness of the trunk with its residual exhaust fumes.

The goons said nothing. Fleming eyed them coldly. *If looks could kill and all that. Stay calm. Do it for Betsie.*

One of the goons lifted him out of the trunk and placed him on the ground. Fleming couldn't support himself even sitting up. He settled on his back. The ground was hard concrete. They were at the top of a circular driveway in front of a large house. It was made out of what looked like red brick with white columns. The sun was almost up, but the blazing fireball in the sky was hidden behind the structure.

In the center of the yard was a well-kept lawn and a tall tree.

Fleming filed away the details and lay still on the ground. They might serve him well, they might not, but at least it kept his mind occupied.

And then he heard the screaming.

Muffled screams, but screams nonetheless, as the goons lifted Betsie out of the trunk and she struggled against their grip, her mouth covered with the same gag as Fleming, her wrists and ankles similarly bound as well. A weight fell from Fleming's shoulders. She was alive. She was pissed. She wasn't going to let the goons off the hook.

They placed her on the ground beside Fleming and their eyes met. Betsie's were wide, wet; Fleming tried to communicate calm. She must have sensed his intention, because she settled down, only breathing hard, as the trunk lid was slammed shut and the car pulled away from them.

That left one goon. He pulled Fleming to his feet and told him to stand still. Fleming's legs felt weak, but he complied. Then the front door opened and two people descended the porch steps. One man. One woman. Fleming recognized the man as Amadis Noguera. There was no mistake. The woman he didn't know, but he had an idea. Stiletto had wanted to know who took over for Giles Flynn. The answer was: his wife.

"Death comes gift-wrapped," said the woman.

The gag muffled Fleming's grunt.

The woman approached him with her arms folded. She had long brown hair, and no amount of makeup could hide the post-50 lines on her face. She eyed Fleming coldly.

"You're the one who ordered the murder of my husband."

Fleming stared at her.

"I don't know if you're lucky or worse off than before," the woman said. "We failed to kill your assassin at the hotel, so he's coming here. Alone, because the two women are dead. Or something. I wasn't clear on that." She glanced sharply at Noguera. Back to Fleming. "We're arranging a nice reception for him. He will meet enough firepower that none of his clever tricks will save him from me putting a bullet in his back. I'll let you watch. And then I'll kill you both."

She said to the goon, "Cut off the ankle ties so they can walk. Take them inside. Put them in the library."

Plenty of improvised weapons there.

The goon used a knife to slice off the bedsheet wrapped around their ankles and shoved Fleming forward. He walked unsteadily past the widow Flynn, Betsie quick-stepping to keep up with him, but losing her balance. The goon grabbed her and helped her stay upright.

Climbing the porch steps wasn't as hard as he thought it would be.

The goon brought them into the well-appointed library. There were no windows. *Probably why it was chosen.* The goon set two high-backed chairs of highly polished wood back-to-back and forced the Flemings to sit, then used a proper rope to tie them together. Their wrists remained bound. As an afterthought, the goon roughly yanked out the gags. Betsie let out a startled cry as her gag was pulled. The goon smiled and waved as he left the room. That's when Fleming noticed the other man standing near the door, more highly polished oak that matched the chairs. He was clean-cut, wore pressed clothes, and a shoulder holster with an automatic pistol nestled under his arm.

Betsie said, "Oh my God, Isaac, what's happening?"

She sounded breathless. Panicked.

Telling her to calm down would only make her state of mind worse. Fleming tried another path. "Stiletto's on his way," he said.

"You heard that woman!"

"She doesn't know Scott the way I do."

Fleming turned to the guard, who grinned a little and shook his head. The guard leaned against the wall now, his arms folded. He looked very satisfied that the captives he was placed in charge of were firmly secured. He also looked like he belonged in a 1970s cigarette ad and Fleming stifled the urge to laugh. He wouldn't be able to explain to Betsie what he found funny.

"I'll tell him to kill you last," Fleming told the man instead.

The guard shrugged.

The door opened again, slowly, the hinges not letting out a single squeak. He felt a draft from the outer hallway. Another woman stepped inside.

She was younger than the widow Flynn. A tall Hispanic with long dark hair and some bruising on her face that was well along the way to being fully healed. She glanced at the guard but said nothing to him. The guard nodded at her. The woman approached Fleming. She smiled.

"We finally meet."

The hairs on the back of Fleming's neck perked up. He said nothing in reply.

"Finally," she said, "I meet the man who has been causing so much trouble for my brother. You're lucky I'm here, do you realize that?"

Fleming knew exactly who she was. *His insider.* They weren't done for yet. He knew why Gabriella Noguera Suarez wanted to remove her brother. In the days leading up to the original CIA mission in Colombia, his agents had actively encouraged her to turn on Amadis because he killed their father.

"I am lucky indeed," Fleming said.

Gabriella laughed. She pivoted on a heel, her long hair trailing behind her, and left the library. Fleming glanced at the guard. He wasn't interested. He was examining a sculpture in a corner.

"What was that about?" Betsie said.

"Quiet, hon."

He wanted to turn and look at her, but their seating position made that impossible. The straight back of the chair was high enough to block any view even if he could. The hard seat had no contour and that contributed to the throbbing ache in his lower back. His arms and shoulders were already numb. He imagined Betsie was in a similar state of discomfort.

"Dammit, Isaac, don't you shush me at a time like this!"

Fleming replied with: "Stiletto is on his way, Betsie. Just wait. Just trust me."

CHAPTER FIFTY-THREE

No safety net. No back-up. No "eye in the sky". Scott Stiletto was alone.

And not for the first time.

A morning assault wasn't what he wanted. Night time would be better. But he didn't have the time for such luxuries as deciding when to unleash whoop ass on the enemy. They had General Ike and his wife somewhere in that house. He didn't think they'd be harmed yet; Barbara Flynn and Amadis Noguera would want to make a show of shooting the three of them at once. Stiletto at least had *that* going for him, assuming he survived the fight against the goons spread out along the property.

He watched the house through a pair of binoculars from the top of a nearby hillside. The grass below him was lush and green and still wet from morning dew.

A gate covered the entrance to driveway of the brick house, a wrought-iron fence encircled the property, and it was isolated enough to provide plenty of combat stretch.

The neighbors might hear gunfire and explosions, sure, and the cops would be on the way midway through the fight, no mistake, but he had enough room to work with. He could blast his way in and out. Hopefully with General Ike and his wife in tow.

He examined the gate at the driveway. His super-charged Tahoe was equipped with armor and countermeasures against attacks. Steel spikes contained in the rear of the vehicle could be spread out on the ground. Tear gas canisters attached to the chassis could spread eye-stinging fumes over the entire yard. The windows had gun ports. Stiletto started counting the number of troops in the front yard and put a plan together.

Who was in there besides Noguera and Barbara Flynn? Had the American mercenaries escaped Colombia too? Maybe they had gone their own way once they realized Noguera wasn't going to get them anywhere, that his cartel network had been crushed. It was a nice thought. Stiletto tossed it aside like the rubbish he figured it was. They were in there, all right.

Maybe even Noguera's sister.

She'd probably want a re-match.

Stiletto grinned.

The trees and flowers lining the inside of the surrounding fence proved to be a challenge for the Flynn guard force. As Stiletto's Tahoe raced up the road heading for the gate, the troops reacted to what was obviously an attack. They fired automatic weapons through the trees and flowers and fence, but only a few of the rounds actually struck the armored Tahoe. Stiletto heard the thumps and paid no mind. His eyes were on the main gate.

Two troopers ran to the gate to shoot through the gaps in the steel bars, the muzzles of their automatic weapons flashing even in the light of the sun. The rounds scored direct hits on the windshield, but bounced off like deflected insects. Stiletto kept the pedal down. The souped-up supercharged 5.3 V8 engine growled.

Scott had lowered both rows of rear seats to give him a flat area in which to move and fire through the window gun ports. All he had to do was climb over the center console seat to get there after launching the tear gas. A mask that would protect him from the residual fumes entering the vehicle sat on the passenger seat.

When the mob gunmen at the gate realized their bullets were doing nothing to stop the onrushing Tahoe, they pivoted to run. One of them made it. The other fell under the wheels of the Tahoe as Stiletto crashed through the gate, the metal twisting and groaning as it was ripped out of its anchor, the gunman who thought he was free and clear getting clipped by a portion of the flying gate which put him flat on the ground.

Stiletto picked up the M-4 from his lap. The weapon was set for full-auto, and the gun port in the driver's side window was open and letting in a rush of air. Stiletto jammed the muzzle through and pulled the trigger with his right hand while steering with his left.

Four covered switches were on the top of the dashboard. Those safety covers had to be flipped up to gain access to the switches that activated the chassis-mounted tear gas and steel spikes. He flicked the switch for the spikes and left the driveway for the center grass, avoiding the tree, the Tahoe's fat tires digging into the landscape and leaving long ruts in the grass. He spun the wheel, turning the car in a long circle, then another turn, checking the rearview for bright winks in the grass indicating where the spikes had fallen.

He kept the trigger back on the M-4 at the same time. The flashing muzzle passed over Flynn gunmen as they rushed for cover or stayed in the open to foolishly fire on the Tahoe. Already some of the men were stepping on the spikes, falling onto others, their clothes spotted red and their shrieks almost overpowering the chatter of the M-4.

The 30-round magazine emptied in seconds. Stiletto winced as he rested the hot weapon on his lap and spun the wheel some more, spinning the Tahoe until the back-quarter panel on the passenger side collided with the tree trunk.

The sudden stop jolted Scott, but he'd been prepared for the impact, and his seatbelt held. He unbuckled, slapped a new magazine into the M-4, then pulled the gas mask over his head and secured it to his face. The rubber seals held tight. Bullets thumped into the Tahoe's body, as ineffectual as ever, and Stiletto glanced around, watching three gunmen boldly approach as if they had the quarry cornered.

Time for tear gas. He flipped up each of the remaining switch overs in quick succession, then hit the activation toggles. As he clumsily climbed out of the driver's seat to the flat area in the back, a plume of white surrounded the Tahoe, rapidly growing as high as the vehicle's roofline.

Stiletto opened the gun ports on both sides of the Tahoe. Gas trickled in. The mask kept him immune. He fired half a magazine out one port, then moved on his knees to the other, and fired out the rest of the ammunition. Coughing and screaming answered the gunfire and gas.

Stiletto reloaded again as the cloud of gas moved away from the Tahoe and began its spread along the property, the drifting cloud still thick as the canisters below the vehicle emptied. When the last of the gas had released, the cloud now moving in all directions, Stiletto pushed open the rear gate and jumped onto the grass to take the fight to whoever remained standing.

CHAPTER FIFTY-FOUR

Stiletto pivoted to face the three approaching gunmen, the M-4 bucking against his shoulder. He moved the muzzle to each target, the men dropping in a bloody pile.

Stiletto breathed hard through the gas mask, the tear gas cloud clearing, gunners around him still yelling from spike wounds or coughing from the gas. Two shooters were camped near the front door, hiding behind the white columns holding up the overhang, and Stiletto fired a burst. The salvo chewed into the front door. Scott next triggered the M320 grenade launcher mounted under the M-4's barrel, the resulting fiery blast wiping out both gunners and turning the porch to rubble.

The door had flung off its hinges, giving Stiletto a clear approach to the inside. He bolted for the door, slapping a new magazine into the M-4, ripping off the gas mask midway. Climbing over the debris and bodies, he launched through the opening, landing on tiled floor.

A spiral staircase directly ahead; off to the right, a

sitting room; to the left, closed doors. One of the doors opened and in came a man with a pistol. Scott swung the M-4 his way and fired two single shots. Both struck the gunner high in the chest and he fell back into the room.

Somebody in the room shouted, "Scott!"

Fleming's voice.

Stiletto stopped at the door, peeked in. He spotted the restrained couple, but no other shooters. Stepping over the gunman's body, he hurried to the General and his wife.

"Are you two hurt?"

Betsie whimpered.

Fleming said, "Just numb."

Stiletto used his Ka-Bar knife to slice the restraints, Fleming and his wife awkwardly embracing while he collected the dead gunner's automatic. It was a Beretta, Model 92 vintage, and he checked the magazine. Full. He handed the gun to the General.

"Get to the garage and find a car," Stiletto said. "If I don't show up after a reasonable amount of time, get out of here."

He turned for the door. The General said nothing further.

Scott stepped over the dead gunner's body again and started across the entry way for the sitting room, soft couches and glass coffee tables on plush carpet with paintings on the wall, white the predominant color, which would go well with blood spatter should he encounter any shooters. The room was divided into the sitting area and a dining table.

A swing door on the other side of the room appeared foreboding. What was on the other side, and who might be hiding there? Stiletto reloaded the M320 with another high-explosive charge and grabbed a vase. He tossed out the flowers and water, then rolled the vase across the carpet. It bumped the door enough to start an inward swing. A burst of automatic gunfire answered the movement.

Stiletto grabbed one of the chairs from the dining table and shoved. The chair pushed the door open some more, coming to a stop, keeping the door wedged. Another burst of auto fire. Stiletto ducked behind a couch and fired the M320. The grenade sailed through the opening to explode on the other side. The swing door buckled from the force of the blast, spider cracks nearly splitting the wall.

Stiletto approached cautiously, probing the opening with the M-4. He stepped over the wrecked chair and door and looked at the two bodies on the floor of the demolished kitchen. Two men. One was in such a bloody state, Stiletto saw no identifying features. But the other was a different story. He recognized the white hair of Edward Kasson, American mercenary and CIA drug smuggling expert. What was left of the man mingled with the other, which probably meant Ross was taken off the board as well.

Stiletto backed out of the kitchen and made his way to the staircase, but stopped short and dived to the sitting room floor as gunners from outside, recovered from the gas, appearing unharmed by the steel spikes, swept into the entryway.

Single shots fired at Stiletto smacked into the furniture and the wall behind him. He fired around the back of a couch, one of the gunners falling, another slipping on his spilled blood as he tried to approach. The third made it all the way. Scott rose, meeting the man as he entered the room, the M-4 flashing again as Stiletto emptied the magazines.

The gunner's forward momentum carried him further into the room, until he struck the glass coffee table, falling onto the top, the glass shattering under the weight of his corpse.

Scott let the empty M-4 hang from its sling. He tore out the .45 and crossed to the gunman who'd slipped in the blood, who was trying to get back on his feet and deploy his weapon. Too late. Stiletto pumped a .45 slug through his head and left him there.

Putting the .45 away and reloading the M-4 once again, Scott took the stairs. He ascended slowly, keeping eyes and muzzle on the upper landing. He stopped. A shadow on one of the walls appeared to have human form. He waited.

Whoever the person was, the wait took its toll. A young woman aimed a pistol around the corner, Stiletto triggering a burst from the M-4 that punched through the wall she hid behind. She let out a yell and fell. Then another woman started screaming. Stiletto raced up to the landing.

He stepped over the first girl, who was quite dead, and aimed at the other, who might have been her twin. *The Flynn daughters.* The second woman had her hands up, her clothes splattered with his sister's guts, and Stiletto moved forward, popping two single shots into the other girl, neck and head. He raced by as her body fell.

The hallway seemed to stretch forever. Where was he going? Who was next? Stiletto kept the M-4 tucked into his shoulder. The next attack might come from anywhere.

CHAPTER FIFTY-FIVE

Amadis Noguera wiped sweat from his brow and then transferred the stainless Smith & Wesson automatic to his left hand so he could wipe his sweaty right hand on the back of his jeans.

If he noticed his sister staring at him, he gave no indication.

They knew from Kasson that only one man was attacking the house, and so far, he had survived the troops outside and, by the sound of it, was tearing through the interior as well. Kasson and Ross had a code word to shout should they take out the attacker, but as Noguera waited, he didn't hear the code word. The walkie-talkie on the floor beside him also remained silent. Kasson had its mate. He and Ross had gone downstairs to deal with the problem, but all Noguera heard was the pulse pounding in his head. All he felt was his rapid heart rate.

They were at the end of the hall on the second floor, the room almost an attic, with the slanted ceiling above indicating how close they were to the roof. There was not enough room to stand. Noguera, Gabriella, and Barbara Flynn were on their knees on the carpet. The only doorway, slightly below floor level, accessed by a steep set of steps, offered a very small slice of the hallway to watch.

Barbara Flynn, clutching her own pistol, crouched at the wall ahead of Noguera, with Humberto beside the doorway steps with an automatic rifle. Humberto's gaze was intent on the doorway. Barbara Flynn was sweating as much as Noguera. Probably thinking about her kids down below. And their current status. Noguera couldn't relate. He glanced at Gabriella. She was on her knees to his left. She was looking at him.

"What is it?"

"Do you think I'd never find out?"

Noguera frowned. "Find what?"

Humberto looked at him too.

"Find what?" Noguera repeated.

"That you killed our father."

Barbara Flynn said, "What's happening?"

"My sister has funny ideas."

"I know *everything*, Amadis. You murdered our father to take his place."

"You might think you know everything," Noguera said. "You might also think you've been fooling me all this time."

Humberto turned from Noguera and faced Gabriella.

Her eyes widened.

"Humberto's been telling me your moves all along."

Gabriella's cheeks flared red as she started to fire her weapon, but Humberto's rifle spoke first, a short chatter, and Gabriella's lifeless body flopped back.

Barbara Flynn didn't leave her spot, but her ferocious eyes bored into Noguera. "What are you doing!"

"Loose end," Noguera said.

Humberto lowered his rifle and faced the doorway again.

Stiletto dodged left, resting against the hallway wall on his left, as the burst of auto fire echoed. Voices followed. Shouting. A woman and a man.

Stiletto opened the breech on the M320 grenade launcher. Empty. He reached for another high explosive grenade, but found the loops on his combat vest empty. No more grenades. And the magazine in the M-4 was also his last. If he ran out of ammo, he'd be down to only his Colt pistol.

He advanced. A narrow doorway at the end of the hall led to a small storage area, but another door immediately to the left revealed carpeted steps. That's where they had to be hiding. Stiletto moved out to the middle of the hallway and held the M-4 tight. Somebody at the top of the steps saw him, shouted an alarm, and sighted down the barrel of an automatic rifle. The M-4 flashed and the head above the gun vanished in a splash of red. A woman yelled. Stiletto noticed the action on the M-4 locked back. He'd had fewer rounds than he thought. He let the M-4 drop to the floor and grabbed the Colt .45 in a two-hand grip.

Somebody else, the female, probably Barbara Flynn, grabbed the dead man's rifle and screamed as she let the magazine go. Stiletto moved to the left wall again. The angle of her firing sent the stream of stringers into the carpet, nowhere near him. When the shooting stopped, Stiletto moved forward, the .45 up and ready. One shot took Barbara Flynn out, and then Stiletto was up the steps, Noguera in his sights, the drug thug rising only to bump his head on the low ceiling.

Stiletto put two rounds dead center in his chest. The kingpin hit the carpet with his face twisted in agony. *So long, Noguera.* Stiletto shot him in the head. Lights out.

He swung the pistol on the other body in the room, the sister. He recognized her. But she'd already been shot. Stiletto didn't have time to ponder why.

Pistol in hand, Scott ran back along the length of the hallway and to the stairs. It took opening a few doors on the ground floor to find the garage, and he almost tripped over another body as he went through the doorway.

Fleming said to Betsie, "Can you walk?"

She nodded. Her eyes were wet, her face blanched, and she was shaking. Fleming checked the gun Scott had given him. He still felt the pins-and-needles effect of his limbs coming back to life, and he couldn't get a strong grip on the Beretta. But soon that would change.

Betsie's eyes landed on the gun.

"Are you—"

"Only if I have to. Come on."

They stopped at the doorway. More shooting in the house from upstairs. Betsie stayed behind him, turning her face away from the dead body on the floor. Fleming knelt beside the dead man. He wore a spare magazine pouch on his belt opposite where the Beretta had been holstered. Fleming grabbed a spare magazine for the gun and pocketed it.

"Step over him."

"Isaac—"

"It's the only way!"

She did what he told her and they started checking doorways for a garage, finding the garage two doors down from the library.

A gunman in the garage pivoted to face them.

"Hey!"

The gunner's weapon came up at the same time Fleming lifted the Beretta. Betsie screamed. Fleming fired twice. The gunner dropped onto the concrete floor.

The echo of the shots bounced off the walls as Fleming grabbed Betsie's left hand and pulled her from the doorway. They had a succession of cars to choose from, sedan to supercar, and Fleming chose a silver four-door

Mercedes.

"Where are the keys?"

Betsie looked stunned as she stared at him.

Fleming told her to stay put and went back to the doorway. On the wall next to the door was a board with keys hanging on pegs. He looked at the Mercedes' license plate, and matched it with a key fob on the board. He helped his wife into the passenger seat and told her to buckle up. He slid behind the wheel and set the fob in the center console. Pressing the engine start button, the motor rumbled to life.

Fleming left the car in park.

"Let's go!" Betsie shouted.

"We have to wait for Scott."

Betsie sucked air sharply.

Stiletto examined the body in the garage and let out a sigh of relief. It wasn't Fleming or his wife.

A horn honked. Fleming waved from inside a silver Mercedes. Stiletto ran to the vehicle and jumped into the back seat.

"Let's go."

Fleming hit the gear selector and pulled out of the parking space, speeding down the length of the large garage to the automatic doors. He slowed as a sensor on the garage wall linked with another sensor in the car and the automatic door slid upward. Fleming powered into the mid-morning sunlight.

Betsie gasped again and again as the carnage in the yard. Fleming regarded the sight with a bored glance or two. Stiletto kept looking for surviving stragglers. He saw none.

He looked at Betsie Fleming. She had both hands over her mouth as she looked around, her eyes wet. She didn't look at her husband or Scott.

Scott sat back and cleared his throat.

Mission accomplished.

Finally.

CHAPTER FIFTY-SIX

Lincoln Memorial
Washington, DC
Two Days Later

"How is Beth doing, General? She took a pretty good smack on the head."

Stiletto and Fleming sat on the steps of the Lincoln Memorial with the statue of Abraham Lincoln looming behind them.

"Doing well. Concussion, of course. Some blood loss from that bullet graze. She'll be back on her feet in no time."

"And your wife?"

Fleming had been chatting up a storm, and Stiletto sensed he wanted to avoid the question.

"Still in a bit of shock," Fleming said without hesitation, "but she's doing better with rest. I think the reality of my job finally hit her."

"Can't blame her."

"Certainly not."

The Reflecting Pool stretched before them, the World War II and Washington Memorials also in sight. Bright blue sky above. It was a peaceful scene compared to the chaos they'd left behind two days earlier.

"There he is," Stiletto said.

Number One, in his usual dark suit, stopped at the steps to the memorial.

"If you think my old bones can carry me up these steps, you are mistaken."

Fleming and Stiletto laughed as they stepped down to meet the older man, who suggested they walk along the memorial circle and have their conversation.

Fleming had been tight-lipped about his decision to resign. Or not. Stiletto wasn't sure what he was going to do. With Number One between them, they started walking, mingling with the tourists spread around the mall.

"Thank you for coming, Edward."

"My pleasure, Isaac."

"Hang on," Stiletto said. "I thought your first name was *Number*."

Number One laughed. "Only a few people are privy to my real name, Mr. Stiletto. My name is Edward Northwood."

"Ah," Stiletto said.

"Please keep it—"

"The vault is sealed, sir."

"Now, Isaac. You have something to talk about?"

"I need to hand in my resignation, sir."

Stiletto winced. His heart dropped into his stomach.

"I won't accept it, Isaac."

"But Edward—"

"Keep walking. I need the exercise. Let me tell you a story, Isaac. You should pay attention, too, Mr. Stiletto. Were either of you with the CIA when the Aldrich Ames case broke?"

"Before my time, sir."

"I was still in the army," Stiletto said.

"I was in the middle of that fiasco," Number One said. "We had a similar case of needing to prove something, Isaac. We needed to prove that we could contain a leak that was costing lives, the lives of a lot of brave Russians who were spying for us. We followed the evidence, until it started leading us into our own home. Then we looked for any excuse not to look around our home, because to admit that the mole was right next to us was too much to admit. Do you know what happened?"

"I have an idea," Fleming said.

"More people died because we weren't willing to admit that one of our own had turned. Between Ames and Hansen at the FBI, we might have lost the Cold War. I don't think enough people realize that."

"The thought has occurred to me more than once," Fleming said.

"All that to say," Number One continued, "that I understand your anger at being dismissed from the CIA. It is perfectly natural. I understand you needing to prove something. You were so focused in other areas that in your emotional state, you forgot the basics of our trade. You made a mistake."

"People died."

"A mistake is forgivable, Isaac. What we did during the hunt for Ames, not so much. It still keeps me awake. We purposefully turned our heads from the truth. I can forgive your missteps; I'm not so sure I can forgive my own."

Number One let out a breath and looked at Fleming. Stiletto watched the two men as they casually strolled. Fleming's eyes were straight ahead. He looked sad.

"That is why I am not accepting your resignation, Isaac. There's still a lot of fight in you, and we frankly need your expertise."

Fleming said nothing.

"Do you really want to quit?"

"Deep down, no."

"Then summon that feeling from deep down and let's get back to work. You won't make the same mistakes again. Next time, you'll remember the cold efficiency with which we are supposed to get our tasks accomplished."

Fleming nodded. His shoulders straightened. "Very good, sir."

"Any thoughts, Mr. Stiletto?"

"I could use a beer."

Number One finally stopped walking to let out a laugh. He grabbed both men by the shoulders. "A beer sounds wonderful. My treat."

Neither Stiletto or Fleming argued.

"And while we enjoy the beer," Number One said, "we need to discuss one last dangling loose end."

"The lawyer," Stiletto said.

"Yes. Adam Rockwell needs to face his reckoning."

New York City

Adam Rockwell snored in his bed.

Stiletto slipped quietly into the bedroom. He held a cylindrical container that held a hypodermic needle. Lock picks and an alarm code obtained by the gee whiz crew at the Zurich HQ of the Trust gave him access to the high-rise condo.

Stiletto opened the container and slipped out the hypo. The transparent tube contained a clear liquid. With his thumb on the plunger, he went around the bed, aimed for Rockwell's exposed arm, and rammed the needle into flesh. Pressed the plunger. The fluid in the hypo rushed into the corrupt lawyer's bloodstream.

Stiletto pulled out the empty hypo as Rockwell jerked awake. Stiletto snapped on the nightstand lamp and stepped back.

"What—!"

Scott held up the hypo. "It will look like a heart attack, counselor."

Rockwell's face blanched.

"You. . .you. . ."

"We have everything we need from you, and the connections you've made with the cartels will start falling. Thanks for your help."

Adam Rockwell, Esq., tried to say more but the drug kicked in. The lawyer's mouth opened; his scream was a choked squeal as he grabbed at his chest. His face tightened and his eyes widened in agony. He fell back on the bed, eyes still open.

Stiletto stood still and waited.

The lawyer did not come back to life. His body lay on the bed like a heavy sack of garbage.

Five minutes later he thumbed Rockwell's eyes closed and switched out the light.

IF YOU LIKED THIS BOOK, CHECK OUT THE DANGEROUS MR. WOLF

MR. WOLF IS A BRAND-NEW HERO THAT YOU CAN ROOT FOR FROM THE AUTHOR OF THE HARD-EDGED SCOTT STILETTO THRILLERS – BRIAN DRAKE.

When innocent people are in the crossfire and the police are unable to help, Wolf picks up where the law leaves off.

As he hunts for clues through the city's dark alleys, chasing mafia killers, solving a decades-old crime, or helping a widow unravel the mystery behind a murder attempt, he quickly uncovers the hidden hands behind the violence, but even he isn't ready for the shocking twists when the last bullets are fired.

THE DANGEROUS MR. WOLF is your introduction to a good man to have on your side.

Better pray he stays there.

AVAILABLE NOW ON AMAZON

ABOUT THE AUTHOR

A twenty-five year veteran of radio and television broad-casting, Brian Drake has spent his career in San Francisco where he's filled writing, producing, and reporting duties with stations such as KPIX-TV, KCBS, KQED, among many others. Currently carrying out sports and traffic reporting duties for Bloomberg 960, Brian Drake spends time between reports and carefully guarded morning and evening hours cranking out action/adventure tales.

Brian Drake lives in California with his wife and two cats, and when he's not writing he is usually blasting along the back roads in his Corvette with his wife telling him not to drive so fast, but the engine is so loud he usually can't hear her.

You will find him regularly blogging at:
www.briandrake88.blogspot.com